Traps

The Iowa Short Fiction Award

Prize money for the award is provided by

a grant from the Iowa Arts Council

Traps

SONDRA SPATT OLSEN

UNIVERSITY OF IOWA PRESS

IOWA CITY

University of Iowa Press, Iowa City 52242
Copyright © 1991 by Sondra Spatt Olsen
All rights reserved
Printed in the United States of America
First edition, 1991

In slightly different forms, "The Butcher's Girl" was first printed in the *Yale Review*, "Harmony" in *Boulevard*, "Working Nights as a Pickle" in *Redbook*, "Topaze" in the *Ontario Review*, "44-28" in the *New Yorker*, "To Forget August" in the *Mississippi Review*, "Gypsy Ways" in *Confrontation*, "Who Could Love a Fat Man?" in *Quarterly West*, "An Old-fashioned Woman" in *Swallow's Tale Magazine*, and "Free Writing" in the *Iowa Review*.

Printed on acid-free paper

The publication of this book is supported by a grant from the National Endowment for the Arts in Washington, D.C., a federal agency.

Library of Congress Cataloging-in-Publication Data
Olsen, Sondra Spatt
Traps/Sondra Spatt Olsen.—1st ed.
p.   cm.—(Iowa short fiction award)
ISBN 0-87745-346-2 (cloth)
I. Title. II. Series.
PS3565.L79T73   1991   91-19062
813'.54—dc20   CIP

Contents

The Butcher's Girl

On the quiet streets of our Brooklyn neighborhood I saw her on my way to school, one of those girls who look like women from far away. I saw the butcher's girl, frightening in her womanliness, advancing slowly upon me along Avenue S. As she drew nearer, her unmistakable shape with its outthrust bosom grew more threatening. She had a face as blank as a coal-chute door and moist, gleaming black eyes; upon her broad red cheek was a small black mole with a hair in it. At this time she was an eighth grader, and I was nine years old.

On other days she appeared in her father's shop sitting on an upturned milk box amid the sawdust and the blood smells. I saw her sometimes carrying out her father's commands, trudging along the sidewalk after school with a large brown bag against her breast. At times I was invisible to her; her cowlike gaze passed over me, and I breathed more freely. At other times she paused and moved closer to me, close enough to brush me with the crackling brown paper. "Where you going?" she said. If I had no ready destination, I felt forced to accompany her, blocks away.

What did she want of me? Not sparkling conversation, for though I could chatter easily, I was silent in her company. Her weighty combination of sex and stupidity rendered me dumb. Also, my own plumpness, an excess of baby fat merely, drew me closer in repulsion to her tremendous flesh.

On this day she approached me hurrying more than normally, her breasts slowly shuttling sideways. Her lips were parted with that mystical look of high rapture. "You busy after school?"

I had a Brownie meeting on Tuesday and a piano lesson on Wednesday, but today was Thursday, and I had not yet learned to lie to save myself.

"Uh, uh."

"I got to take my graduation picture," she said. "I need someone to deliver for me. You get the tips. They're good on Thursday. You ain't got much walking, either."

I allowed myself to breathe because I knew that my mother would never let me ring the doorbells of strange houses. This had been proven at Girl Scout Cookie time as well as at Thanksgiving, when I was not allowed to join the roving bands of costumed kids chanting, "Anything for Thanksgiving?" door to door.

"My mother won't let me."

"Don't tell her."

This was an argument I had never expected. While I grappled with it, she continued, "Just tell her you was helping out after school."

Stupefied by her shrewd certain tone, I agreed, at the same time feeling a dead, sinking helplessness.

"Come right to my father's after school. Don't carry no books."

"What do I do with my books?"

"Leave them in school, but don't leave them in the shop. My father don't want no books in his way. He'll throw them in the fat barrel."

I left my books behind the friendly counter at Harry's Candy Store and entered the butcher's shop at three o'clock like a sacrificial lamb. Herman the Butcher stood in a businesslike way behind his woodblock, his dull cleaver beside him. His ruddy cheeks, red lips, and large white teeth reminded me of steak. It would do me no good with him to say that I had all A's on my report card, that Mrs. Bensen, our English teacher, had read my composition aloud with eloquent praise and then tacked it in the corridor for the whole school to see. If I had felled an ox, he perhaps would smile on me.

"Take these to Mrs. Lipsit, Mrs. Brown, and Mrs. Cunningham. I got the addresses written on the bag. Then come back here. Maybe I got more for you." He wiped his fingers on his rosy apron. "You do good, you can make money when Pearl is away."

I staggered out of the shop. The bell rang sharply behind me before Herman could call me back. "I wouldn't use Herman even for soup bones," my mother had once said with some violence. "He can keep his credit." She shopped for meat at Mr. Ganz, the kosher butcher. "His meat is cleaner."

Mr. Ganz's store on the next block seemed bare rather than clean. Perhaps he was going out of business, for his showcase stood empty except for two or three yellow plucked chickens and some long brown chops. Mr. Ganz himself was thin and nervous with a narrow black mustache. He often smiled gloomily when he came out of the icebox, as if he had seen something to his disadvantage inside.

On the street, my reason returned to me. I read the penciled addresses and plotted a course. If I was clever, I would get home free, and my mother would never know. I would donate my tips to charity, to the Girl Scouts.

Mrs. Lipsit's was easy, only one block over, a corner house with a sun porch. Through the window panels I could see who was coming and run if needed. Mrs. Lipsit herself came to the door, unknown to me but wearing a reassuring frilled apron and tortoiseshell combs in her upswept hair, just like my mother. Just like my mother, she was polite, said "Oh, my goodness" when she realized she had no tip handy and kept me waiting for a long time beside the forest-green sun porch door while she scouted out a dime.

My load and heart were lighter as I slipped along the sidewalk, swinging my fat blond pigtails in play. Mrs. Brown lived three blocks further toward Water Street on the stagnant bay, a fascinating place with huge exposed sewer pipes and a rotten smell—just across the border of my permitted territory.

The Brown house was dark and forbidding, with overgrown hedges that must be breached to reach the side door. The front gate was bound with a padlock—out of the question. The nicked slimy green door held no reassuring window. The bell did or did not ring. I put my ear to the splintery panels to see if I could hear footsteps, and suddenly the surface shifted. I stumbled and looked up, inhaling the sour breath of an old man in a dirty khaki sweater and ragged pants. "Your meat," I said with remarkable aplomb, but the old man only looked at me crooked and banged the door shut.

I reread the paper bag. Herman's scrawl was ugly but unmistakable: 9812 Water Street. I knocked, but no one came. I waited about fifteen minutes, thought about leaving the package leaning up against the moldy green door, looked inside it, saw bulging sausages as well as several other stained parcels, thought better of it, and walked slowly away in despair. There was no point in delivering the third bag; if I had to return to Herman in shame, one undeliverable would be just as bad as two. Rubbing my shin where the hedges had scratched me, I found myself walking in the direction of the bay. I was already done for, I reasoned, so I might as well go down to the water.

I heard wild screams ahead of me. A rowdy gang of boys was playing stickball in an untidy line near the shore on the other side of Water Street. I recognized them without knowing in particular who they were, yet I knew from the silhouettes of their cowlicks and bony shins in rolled up pant legs and sagging socks that these boys were my traditional enemies, just as they knew me by my pigtails and neat Trimfit anklets in my sturdy school shoes. I heard the violence in their shrieked repeated name-calling. In a few moments if I crossed the street, or even perhaps if I didn't, they would chase after me, calling me names and perhaps throwing rocks. I had been hit on the temple by a snowball in February by a boy who had called out cheerfully, "Look at me!"

I kept on walking along Water Street until I came to a street I had never seen before called Blossom. I saw no flower gardens, only a dank row of brick stoops extending back in the direction in which I had come. Clutching my parcels to my light sprigged dimity chest, I slowly and curiously made my way up Blossom Street. The air seemed to be growing darker and damper. Nightfall was coming, or it was about to rain. I pretended I was in my bed, imagining an exciting journey.

The cries of the boys were soon out of earshot. They had never even glimpsed me, and I was safe. I decided to make another stab at delivering Mrs. Brown's meat, but when I came to the intersection which should have shown me Barker Street, the sign said Blackhorn. I wasn't lost, since I was within a block or two of my destination, but I was mystified. What was Blackhorn?

As I pondered, a man came up the street toward me. I was puzzled about him, for he was obviously not a schoolboy or a delivery boy. At that time of day all the grown men were at work; those left were schoolboys, the elderly, or tradesmen. This fellow seemed about college age and very well dressed in a brown-belted jacket and tweed trousers. He wore a cap at a jaunty angle over his fair curly hair. He was singing a popular tune I very much liked: "Now is the hour / When we must / Say good-bye." Just as he came abreast of me and my packages, he stopped and sang "hello" at the point where he should have sung "good-bye." I thought this very witty.

When he said, "May I help you with those parcels, little girl?" I naturally thought of the wolf in Little Red Riding Hood. Nonetheless, for reasons which must have had to do with his snapping blue eyes and the regularity of his straight small nose, I handed my packages to him, and he gave me a smile of the most piercing sweetness. He then began to run away from me as fast as he could go, disappearing at the corner of Water Street and speeding toward the bay, the huge sewer pipes, rowdy boys, and rotten smell.

I continued walking along Blossom Street away from the bay, my face all screwed up to prevent tears falling out of my eyes, and gulping very loudly to force the tears down my throat and into my stomach, and scuffing my shoes with their metal tips very loudly on the sidewalk to cover up my gulping, for crying, I knew, was very stupid. No one stopped me or took any notice of me until I came to a wide shopping street which bore the same name as my shopping street. I thought it might be the same, turned in the right direction, and soon found myself at Herman's Butcher Shop.

On a milk crate in front of the shop, her red hands laced together on her broad stomach, sat Pearl, the butcher's girl, in old black sneakers and a new ruffled white organdy and dotted Swiss graduation dress. Bursting into loud wails, I rushed over to Pearl and threw myself on her mercy, or rather into her lap, right at the spot where her crisp peplum was crushed by her bosom. "I was robbed! A boy stole my packages! What will I tell my mom?"

I could feel the gentle pressure of Pearl's breasts as she leaned over me. She didn't understand what I was saying and made me repeat the message. Then she sat for a long time, blinking. "Don't you worry," she said finally.

She rose and went into the butcher's shop, while I remained kneeling, the sidewalk pressing cruelly into my knees. She returned soon, her black eyes gleaming. "I fixed it with my father," she said. "He does what I say."

"Is he going to make me pay for the meat?"

But Pearl only shook her head. "Don't worry. I fixed it." She sat down again and squashed me into a hug.

As I lay in her lap, embracing her scratchy stomach, being comforted and admired as a helpless baby is admired, I felt for the first time the warmth of unconditional love. It seemed to me I was not so awful, after all. In a moment, the feeling had gone.

"We'll be friends," Pearl said. "I'll walk you home every day. I'll visit you at your house."

I imagined my mother's haughty rolling glance, her scornful stare. My mother's legs were slim in glossy nylons. Her small polished shoes were dainty, her underpants pink and fresh. Everything she did was excellent.

I saw Pearl's bulky entrance through our narrow garden gate, her cracked black sneakers treading our Chinese rug. I heard my mother whisper, "stupid," and also, "piano legs."

How could I bring home such a creature? What would people say? Wouldn't that make me a butcher's child, too?

"No," I groaned, breaking free with difficulty from Pearl's grasp. "Not now." I stood and began to compose myself, patting my eyes. "But thank you very much for your help. Thank you, anyway."

Pearl's black eyes looked duller, like stones. The hair in her little mole, which I had forgotten, sprang to my attention. "You don't have to pay for the meat," she repeated. "I paid for it myself from my tips."

Although I tried to be thankful and said I was thankful, I felt an ugly grating in my heart. I turned and ran.

Until the end of the term I took a long circuitous route to avoid meeting Pearl on my way to school. If I glimpsed her slow advance, I darted down a side street. Once I crouched behind two enormous metal garbage cans in the alley behind the movie house. Once I reversed direction and scooted home, pleading a sudden headache. I never let her get near me again.

In the fall Pearl went safely off to Eastern District High School, where she earned a general diploma. For years after, I saw her strolling along the sidewalk to Harry's for a candy bar or lingering for a smoke near the dusty butcher shop window. Although she gave me a look with a lapidary gleam to it when I could not avoid her, we never spoke.

Harmony

Diamond, the first husband, died in the apartment next door, on the other side of Rose's bedroom wall. The most sensational event of his tenancy and Rose didn't hear a word, slept through it, it was that low-key. According to the night elevator man, the police had shown up with resuscitators much too late and stayed briefly. No widow's weeping penetrated the wall, but then Minky was not the heavy-mourning type.

Diamond had been the owner of a big lamp store, a straight-forward middle-aged businessman. He always took off his hat in the elevator and said good morning to Rose, or good evening. Diamond's successor began as some kind of stud. He didn't go to business in a decent suit and hat but lounged about the apartment much of the day and then went off at mysterious intervals wearing his Adidas and a baseball cap. He greeted Minky loudly at the front door with hugs and kisses. During this premarital period Rose heard every night through the bedroom wall a symphony of grunts and moans. When she glimpsed the perpetrator strutting in the hallway in a gross tight-fitting T-shirt, the coarse black hairs on his chest spilling out, the thigh muscles in his tight jeans rippling along with a life of their own, Rose felt the disgust appropriate to a sixty-year-old widow. When she realized that the pair had married ("Diamond" disappeared from the lobby directory and "Berk" went up), she said to the elevator man on her way to the ninth floor, but in a roundabout way so as not to start any real trouble, "The quality of life on nine isn't getting any better, let me tell you."

The loud sex phase stopped when all at once Diamond's son came back to live at home. This was a boy Rose never took to. He'd grown up and moved away two or three years before, when Rose's husband was still alive. Max had always called him The Lazy. "You'll be surprised to hear that The Lazy is back!" Rose imagined Max's sniffing expression of disdain as she broke the news to him. How Max would snort!

No kid, Ricky Diamond couldn't be all that much younger

than Berk. Instead of working, he too hung around the house all day singing and playing his guitar, both poorly because he couldn't grasp the principles of harmony. He sounded like a wounded animal when he howled out his melodies, mainly Dylan and Simon and Garfunkel hits from the sixties. He also played the harmonica with a lonesome sound that Rose liked. Once in a while Minky would join in with her showy soprano. Whenever his mother kept him company in a song, Ricky's voice would magically improve.

Berk always spoke politely to Diamond's son, but Rose's sensitive ears could detect a note of exasperation or repulsion when he asked after Ricky's practice session or offered Ricky his pancake because he was too full. Their dinner table stood on the terrace right next to Rose's kitchen window. Her neighbors with their loud, unmodulated voices often sounded as if they were sitting at her kitchen table. Berk in particular took prizes for loudness where the competition was stiff.

When cold weather arrived and the Berks moved indoors, Rose almost missed them. For a time she heard nothing. Was Ricky still with them? Berk? Was anybody next door at all?

Somebody must be in residence because packages left outside the door were always taken in. Some days someone was cooking up a storm in the kitchen; Rose smelled that good onion-frying smell in the hall. Berk had taken up gourmet cooking maybe?

Without warning, a new telephone extension began ringing in Rose's life. Calls in the bedroom next door began pouring in on a new type of phone, not the telephone company's familiar ring but a pleasant, frolicsome chirping. Rose would pull up a comfortable chair to the wall and put her feet on the bed.

"As you know, we're having some problems. . . . I knew the kind of man he was when I married him. . . . What are friends for if not to tell troubles to?"

Minky sounded so depressed that Rose felt bad for her. She'd never cared for Minky, even in the days when she'd said hello. Minky still went out to business in the lamp store, but unlike Rose who had done part-time secretarial work for her husband, sending out bills, posting, doing the deposits, Minky was a creative presence. She actually bought lamps for the store and twice a year went on business trips to Italy. Minky had her hair done every Friday at the Phaisant D'or on Kings Highway and always went out on weekends smelling of perfume and sporting what looked to be real gold jewelry. Rose surmised that Minky had already begun something with Berk before Diamond died, or how else would she have gotten started so fast?

Now that Minky was not getting along, Rose thought of laying in wait for her by the elevator just to offer sympathies. But it wouldn't do. You never mixed in before, she thought, and it's not right to mix in now.

Another bombshell: Rose monitored a series of calls one afternoon from Berk to real estate agents. Usually he talked to bookies and poker players. He had a suave telephone voice, sounding like the sort of low-key, well-educated fellow you'd love to have as a neighbor. He transformed himself in these calls. Rose could barely keep her ear to the wall when she discovered that Berk was actually looking to buy a co-op apartment in Manhattan. Ocean Parkway in Brooklyn wasn't good enough for him? Rose heard him say to one agent, "This place is luxurious but too cramped. We can't even have guests" (he meant Ricky) "without their being on top of us. Also I want a place that isn't noisy."

Rose felt fury. Here was the loudest mouth in the borough having the nerve to complain about other people's noises. As if she, Rose, ever made the slightest peep—living alone, never having company, walking around in house slippers for fear of making too heavy a footfall. Now Rose recollected that once, months ago, she had fallen asleep in front of the television and this loutish Berk had come by to ask if she could please turn it down.

If Max were alive, he'd complain to these obnoxes. Rose wasn't feeling strong enough to complain. What was she supposed to say? Cut down on the sex? Shut your traps at the table? Max had been a model person, an artist, a furrier, not some stevedore. He never raised his voice. Instead of living off his wife, he took care of her. He left Rose enough so she didn't have to work any more. Once a month she went to the Chem-Bank vault and clipped the municipal bond coupons Max had so thoughtfully provided. Everything was neatly arranged in brown envelopes marked January–July, February–August, plus folding scissors from Hofritz, Max's last gift.

Such good care Max took of her. What a man for peeling an orange, and how he cut up grapefruits for her in tiny sections, just so, with his golden hands. How neatly he would rinse out the milk containers and fold them in little squares, tie up newspapers in stacks with sturdy rope. He would clean her reading glasses, clicking his tongue and wiping them with a delicate square of tissue from his wallet. "How can you see?" he'd say. Even now Rose turned to him; when the jam jar top wouldn't open and her hands wouldn't work right, she would implore, "What now, Max? Help me!" She would hear his sensible voice saying, "Put margarine on the toast, Rosale. Forget the jam."

Yes, Rose was glad she was going to hear the last of her vulgar neighbors. Let them move to Park Avenue if they so desired. On the other hand, it was possible that new people beyond these cardboard walls would be worse than the Berk family and son by a previous marriage. Instead of three, there might be six. Instead of one guitar, a family of mezzo-sopranos practicing scales every morning. A family with barking dogs or the ultimate fate, infants.

Things could be worse, Rose reasoned. Although the Berks passed her right by in the hall as if she were air, new tenants might be overfriendly, pestering her night and day to borrow expensive brown sugar and cream of tartar or wrecking her cannister vacuum cleaner as had once happened long ago. Sherm Berk, though an obnox, was a stable obnox. For every late poker game he threw on his terrace, there was another evening when he was entirely away from home. Rose began to have second thoughts.

She had a hard time, though, piecing together news about the projected move. Rose tried applying a glass to the wall. She could hear Minky saying, "Two hundred sixty-eight thousand—they have a lot of nerve!" But was Rose to deduce that this was the price of a co-op apartment?

Meanwhile, Minky Berk was undergoing stress. Through the wall her voice quavered. Glimpsed in the elevator, she looked haggard. Even her champagne blond hair was a different shade, watered down. She had only herself to blame, of course. If she had asked Rose's opinion—should I marry this brute—this coarse-speaking gambler? Shall I legitimize my carnal passions? Rose could have helped her avoid tragedy. But since Berk, Minky had never acknowledged Rose's existence with even a nod.

Rose's scenario: Berk would force Minky to abandon her cherished nest in Brooklyn for some opulent place (Diamond's estate paying the bills), and then when she was adrift in an unpleasant neighborhood full of snobs, he'd abandon her or abuse her till she left him. She'd be out a husband and a reasonable apartment with terrace. Perhaps then she'd long for her tranquil old life-style and her tranquil old neighbor, Rose Levine.

One day her own phone rang in her own bedroom, and at first Rose didn't even notice. It was her sister, Ruth, inviting her to see a Broadway show.

Rose declined. "I can't stand being stepped on by all those people in Times Square. The subway is too much for me."

"So take a car service. Max didn't leave you enough?"

"Thank you, Ruthie, no. I just don't have the energy."

"You're still depressed? Don't you think you should snap out of it?"

"I should, yes, of course I should, but since when does a depressed person have strength?"

"I'll call you at Thanksgiving," Ruth said. "There's always a place for you at our table. We're not having a turkey this year because Art is on a special diet, and both girls are bringing their new companions, so we'll be crowded, but we'll be glad to have you if you care to come."

That evening came an incredible uproar, shattering yells, a fusillade of shrieks. Ricky's simple voice insisting, "I was here first!" Minky protesting, "Don't you dare humiliate my son!" Berk yelling, "You don't own me!" The apartment rocked. "Make up your mind who you care for!" "You think my life is a crap game you can walk in and out of?" "I was here first!" Rose wouldn't have been surprised to hear shots fired. She noted the time on her digital just in case.

After the blow up—silence, endless unsettling silence. Disturbed, Rose longed for some ordinary commotion. I'm too old to get involved in this kind of affair, she thought. What are they to me except shadows with voice boxes? She began to feel slightly faint from stress and curiosity. Maybe I should move to Florida while I can still make the adjustment. But the warm tropical weather, all those open windows and patios. Whose life will I be dragged into there? What tumults and passions? What if I'm not dragged anywhere?

By Friday she began to feel panic. The people next door had already moved or murdered each other. Only a grave could be more silent. She thought she could hear a quartz clock ticking on the other side of the wall. The word I want is "spastic," she thought. Drastically spastic, the whole affair. Beyond the usual. She was talking to herself.

With life-giving relief Rose at last heard a chirping ring and

Minky's unabashed loud voice. "He wanted to move on my money. . . . God forbid I should think again of marrying a younger man. I don't care what the trend is now, it's madness."

"That's what she says now," Rose thought with satisfaction. "But let another lummox with a tan come by. You don't have to be sixty to recognize a woman who needs it bad."

That night while puttering around the bedroom in her flowered housecoat, Rose suddenly heard Berk's grunts and moans coming through the bedroom wall. Rose heard Minky's animal cry of satisfaction. Then Rose felt a warning signal, a dizziness, a blankness in her ears. She had to sit down on the bed and loosen her bra.

She looked on the bureau at the silver-framed picture of Max as a young man with his brown hair so neatly parted and his lively reddish brown mustache. "Forget these riffraff," he was saying. "They're not your kind with their vulgar sex life. Remember how I made love to you in the backseat of the La Salle? Did we make noises? Did we disturb the neighborhood?"

"You're right, Max, you're right. Listening in and looking down is no satisfaction for an old lady."

"Better get a dog or a cat quick. Go for long walks. Join the Golden Age Club at the Y." From the silver frame Max gave her a sober look, full of understanding. "Forget about the sex angles. Simmer down, Rosale. Even better, buy earplugs. You're hearing everything next door because you want to hear."

She wasn't fooling Max. No point in trying to fool the dead. He alone of anybody in the world understood that what she wanted was to get into bed with a man of whatever age, just to feel the flesh inside her.

"What the hell did you leave me for, you jackass?" she cried. "I don't want to be old and alone."

She picked up the picture of Max and threw it with all her

strength against the wall through which the noises came. When the sound stopped abruptly, she threw a ceramic lamp, a silver-backed brush, comb and mirror, and a crystal perfume flask. After making these colossal noises, for just one second Rose felt perfect relief.

Working Nights
as a Pickle

My children were waiting in the hallway with their disguises on. They wanted to surprise their father, but he surprised them first. He never showed up. They waited an hour, a Batman and a Daisy Duck, first poised by the elevator and then sitting sadly on the floor.

It was my fault. I should have told them that their father might not turn up—he's a weak man . . . unreliable . . . he means well.

But how can you say that about someone's *father*? He cares for you, but only theoretically. He can hardly take care of himself, let alone a three-year-old and a six-year-old.

I kept hoping for a train crash: that would be a good reason for him to disappear without a word. Finally the children went to bed docilely. In fact, they were easier to handle than usual. Only one thing—Susie asked for a bottle. She hasn't drunk from a bottle for more than a year. Since before her father left us. David wanted to stay up a little longer—in case Daddy came through. "The Christmas presents finally came, didn't they? Even though it was New Year's?" I told him he could wait better in bed, and after about two minutes he dropped off to sleep.

Once alone, I was filled with a familiar, not unpleasant rage. Anger is always better than depression, I thought. I recalled the furious battles John and I had had when we were still together. How I had thrown a six-foot rubber plant at him (I'm only five feet tall) and how I once locked him out of the apartment in his shorts and he had had to pound and beg until I let him in. At first we always made up, and he would do all the laundry for me to show he still cared—a really good job—all the underwear bleached snowy white and carefully folded and the legs of my jeans unwrinkled and sharply creased. He'd pull them flat with his bare hands to show his good will. Some couples end their quarrels with turbulent sex, but we always had sparkling laundry.

I made a cup of tea and tried to straighten up the apartment.

The new baby-sitter, though warm and motherly, was something of a slob. I sorted out the mixed-up pieces of the Flintstones game from those of Peter Rabbit. While I was crouching on my hands and knees, the telephone rang. It was John.

"Where are you?" I demanded.

"I'm still in Boston."

"Why didn't you call before? The children were crushed. They were standing in the hallway with their Halloween masks on." I hoped to tear his heart with this pathetic detail, but he passed over it.

"Oh, hell—I *told* Bob to call and leave a message. We had a super-express job and I had to work overtime. I couldn't get out of it, couldn't even get to the phone. I've been on overtime all week—dead tired, can hardly see straight."

"You poor thing."

"Well, can I speak with Dave and Susie?"

"They're asleep now. What's wrong with you, John? You know they're asleep by nine. *Hoosh*." The exasperated rush of air from my mouth felt like dragon's breath. When would John ever get back to reality? Had he ever been in it?

"Well, don't be self-righteous about it, Jane. I did try to send a message. Also it won't kill them. I'll come next Saturday morning instead and take them to the Aquarium."

"Okay. They'll enjoy that. But let it be a surprise—I won't mention it."

John's voice rose in his own baffled yelp of exasperation. "A surprise? Why? Think I won't show up?"

"Well, you didn't show up tonight, did you? You left them hanging there, all hopeful, waiting to jump into your arms. They haven't seen you since April and you haven't even sent them a postcard, but for some reason the poor dopes still love you."

"It was unavoidable. I couldn't avoid it. With you, I can never get out from under, can I, Jane? You're always grousing. You never forget."

"Go to hell."

As usual, we both slammed down the receiver at the same moment—our only mutuality. I had forgotten to ask him what time he planned to arrive, but it really didn't matter, did it? He would be late.

All winter I had been looking for another man. I had thought it would be easy—my expectations weren't very high. Some male over thirty. Someone smart. Someone who loved children—no, someone who *could* love children. I had renounced hopes of great romance or sensational sex. After John, anyone steady, someone who didn't slam doors or forget to come home, would be sensational. But I never met anyone even marginally possible. I never met anyone.

I tried to make new women friends. That's the conventional wisdom for separated women—make women friends and they'll lead you to men. But each time I talked to a woman, I'd hear myself whining. With mothers I'd complain that my children were mean to each other. With fellow workers that our boss was mean to us. (When I said my son had chicken pox, my boss said, "Hire a nurse.") I kept reminding myself of my sad mother, who'd whined steadily without result for fifty years and died just after saying, "This pillow is too flat."

For the past two months I'd been taking a gym class on my lunch hour. Since John had left I'd grown slack. Breasts that had been full and firm after the babies had shrunk away to nothing. I thought that exercise might make me more alluring for the beach season and all the possible thirty-year-old males jogging past. But while I always felt physically better after working out, I couldn't stand the other women. Good-looking and carefree, they were executive secretaries, young lawyers, women who ran boutiques. Their talk in the locker room annoyed me—European trips, names of the latest "in" restaurants, but mostly allusions to sexy men.

I consoled myself with the thought that the boyfriends they had wouldn't possibly suit me, but I couldn't help feeling envious, a little old lady, aged thirty, looking for a little old man. I remembered all the well-built young men, garage mechanics and mowers of lawns, whose sunburned flesh I had scorned when I was in high school, and I wished that I had made love with them while it was still possible.

John hadn't always been impossible to live with. We had once been happy, though he'd done a few foolish things, like quitting one job before he was certain he had nailed down another and selling our car to a con man who left town without paying. I believe our turning point came one night when David was two.

I was pregnant and feeling sick, so when John urged me to go out to the movies, I went. When I left, David was asleep and fine. When I returned he had a hoarse, barking cough and a fever of 103. Instead of calling the doctor or even looking up the symptoms in our *Home Medical Aid*, John had been pacing around the living room, holding David in his arms, waiting for me to get home and tell him what to do.

Just as I came in the door David went into a long spasm of coughing from which he couldn't catch his breath. I was so scared that I almost choked myself, but I raced into the bathroom with him and turned on the hot water in the shower. Steam was good for coughing—I remembered reading that from one of the thousand child-care books I read during the long months of my first pregnancy. Within a few minutes David's coughing had ceased, though he was still feverish.

"I knew you'd know what to do," John kept saying joyfully, until I turned on him.

"Why the hell didn't you call the doctor, like a sane person?"

Instead of answering me, he grabbed his coat and ran out the door.

As it happened, when I telephoned the doctor he prescribed a special medicine. If only John had been with me to rush to the all-night drug store! Instead I had to get a cab driver to deliver the prescription, and somehow he went astray. David began another frightening croupy fit. I saw then for the first time that John was no help to me. We didn't speak for a day or two, and when we resumed our ordinary life, it was never the same.

John appeared at our door early Saturday morning, but we hardly recognized him. Since we'd last seen him he had grown a full brown beard that hid his pleasant features and made him look sinister. As a young man his firm rosy cheeks had been one of his most attractive features. What a disastrous idea, I thought.

David and Susie were quiet and shy, and I began to understand why they had worn their Halloween masks the last time. Perhaps the new beard was a disguise, too, though John said he'd just grown tired of shaving.

John sat down in his old chair and good-naturedly offered to let the children pull his beard. "What is yellow, then green, then yellow?"

The children didn't know.

"A banana that works nights as a pickle."

This cracked up David.

"You're wrong," offered Susie stubbornly. "Bananas *don't* work like pickles."

David moved closer to John. "What did one ear say to the other?"

As I stood above them, I had the impression that John looked worn-down and nervous despite his joking, that his bright-blue eyes were tense with some unreadable message. Right after our quarrels John had always been so totally unperturbed. "Why are you so upset?" he would say. This denial of the past always enraged me, so I was glad of his intense looks, whatever they meant.

Because it was going to be the first really hot day of the summer, John suggested going to the beach before the Aquarium.

"Hooray!" the children cried.

"Why don't you come too, Mommy?" John said.

Although I'd been looking forward to a peaceful day alone, I said yes; it was such a pleasure to be wanted by someone over six years old.

As I changed into my bathing suit I could hear the children becoming themselves, beginning to interrupt each other, screaming. I could hear John in his mock-judicial voice saying, "One at a time, now. OK, you first, Dave. . . ." It felt like a family again, chaotic and predictable.

Although I'd been looking forward all winter to the beach, I was pained by the flat gray sand jammed with people and rubbish. I'd remembered it as a golden crescent. The surf, though, was blue and raging. Most people stood waist-deep, letting themselves be slammed about by the waves.

We had a discussion about where to put down the blanket. I preferred a spot further back from the water; John insisted that we'd be cooler down close to the sea. "We can always move if the tide comes up," he said.

I didn't argue. The children were delighted and ran back and forth, ankle-deep in the icy water. I was afraid they'd be knocked down.

"Relax," said John in an indulgent voice I hadn't heard in a long time. "Enjoy yourself. Lie down on the blanket. Let me watch them." And when I took off my jeans and T-shirt he smiled and said, "You're looking great."

Time passed peacefully. John did all the monitoring, scolding, dispensing of justice. When he took the children for hot dogs, I was so relaxed I fell asleep in the sun.

Later on he started them digging holes in the sand; then he came to lie down beside me on the blanket. He had grown thinner and less muscular. His ribs showed; his neck had a crease in it; and with his new beard I might have passed him many times on the beach without recognizing him.

"Why are you staring at me?"

I turned my head away. It was hard to ignore this strange new body only inches away.

John put his hand on the small of my back and gently rubbed it, and I felt a sexual thrill so pure and delicious that it far surpassed, in its insinuating way, the most strenuous foreplay.

"Ummm," I said, and leaned my face against his shoulder.

"It's not working out in Boston," John said in a low voice. "I'm still depressed. I was happier at home with you and the kids."

"What are you saying?"

"That I want to come back."

I didn't know what to reply. I didn't believe people could make a new start without changing in some basic way. But I was lonely, too.

I was about to say this, and I think I was going to add, "But maybe if we had some counseling . . ." when at that moment a giant wave came out of the sea, came out of nowhere, and broke over us. We leaped up fast, but everything we had was ruined.

David and Susie came running, squealing in fright and excitement, as John and I frantically dragged the blanket to higher ground.

"I told you we shouldn't have come so close!" I cried without thinking.

John turned to me in fury. "You bitch!" He grabbed his sopping pants and picked up his soggy shoes. All his possessions were arranged on the blanket, I discovered, as if he had been prepared to run away at any instant. Then he walked off without a word. The children and I stood staring after him in shock.

Now I had to explain with as much charity as possible why their daddy had run off once more without saying good-bye. I knew Susie would cry and that I would promise her ice cream and that as soon as Susie calmed down David would begin to tease her without mercy.

I put my arms around the children and tried to interpret John's fury to them. "Daddy is like a firecracker, and he just explodes. When he gets angry, he runs away. Daddy got mad at me, not you, and he rushed away and left you behind. Later on he'll forget about being angry, and he'll be sorry."

David and Susie seemed to understand this. They nodded.

But I can never forget about my own anger, I should have gone on to explain. I always remember how badly he's treated me, and I always remind him. I knew I could never stop reminding him.

We would go to the Aquarium. While I wrung out our sandy towels and packed them in a shopping bag, I told myself that we weren't any worse off than we had been before, yet somehow I knew that we were.

Topaze

Paulie didn't have to be dragged out of bed that November morning but rushed into the kitchen like light. "Ma," he said, "I can't decide on a girl or a boy."

Sally was frantically making pancakes, shoveling them slap-dash onto paper plates. Everyone had to be on the sidewalk by 8:15 sharp, and Trudy was still in her sleeper, playing with her trucks, and Paul shaving in the bathroom. Although Sally already wore her smartly tailored working clothes and high heels, her uncombed blond hair stood up in strange peaks, like meringue.

"A girl or a boy is fine with me, Paulie," she said, "but it has to be fixed, remember. Connie will help you pick a healthy one. And if they don't have the cat of your dreams at Bide-a-Wee today, you can always go back there next week." Sally gave Paulie a hug, though there wasn't much to hug nowadays. He was mostly bone with many missing teeth.

"I waited a whole year, Ma. I never thought I could." Paulie put his arms around her and planted his nose in her stomach, a wonderfully appealing embrace, though she couldn't help wondering if his nose was perfectly dry.

Sally did not want a pet. Last November when they gave in to Paulie's unremitting pleas for a cat, she had thought life would inevitably be easier the following year. Twelve months later, the family appeared, if anything, a little nearer to chaos, even though Trudy was at last old enough for nursery school and Paulie had learned to read and was able to amuse himself for one whole hour at a time.

At the stove some mornings Sally felt dynamic and powerful, like the village blacksmith or the captain of some heavy industry, but today she felt weak and insubstantial. So many mouths to feed, and pancakes, unlike horseshoes, were gobbled up and gone in an instant.

Sneaking a quick look at the clock, Sally wondered if she had time to call Weather. Better just to look out the window. But up and down the length of their narrow street, mostly garages, warehouses, and tenements, there was not a single person to be seen—not one warmly or lightly dressed. "Look, Paulie," she said, "I'm putting the cat money and the cab money in your buttoned jacket pocket, and don't forget to thank Connie for her help."

Paul stalked through the kitchen with his zombielike morning gait. Sally often thought he didn't really wake up until his face hit the air outside their apartment building. Then his blue eyes would flash in his pale face, and he would say something unexpected, like "Let's try to go skiing this winter" or "Our landlord is a barracuda." She tried not to bother him at breakfast, but he should be warned about the cat. Oh dear God, she so hoped it wouldn't be a nuisance.

"Paul, Paulie's getting his cat today."

"Umm, good." Paul sat down at the table and picked up his knife and fork. "My mother had cats. They're clean, dignified animals." Paul stared at the front page of the *Times* and began eating abstractedly, already back in his dream, as if he'd used up his stock of words for that morning.

Paulie had soaked his pancake with syrup and was now sloshing the pieces around on his plate in his stylized substitute for eating. His mouth was open. "One thing that's worrying me, Ma. If it already has a name, do I have to use it? Even if I don't like it?"

"Well, I don't know. You have to ask Connie. She's the cat expert. I don't know if a cat can learn another name. What name do you want?"

"Minnie."

"So you do want a girl?"

"Or Mickey."

"Nice, both nice." Sally suddenly raced out of the kitchen to the children's room. Trudy was lying on her back on the floor, balancing a truck on the soles of her feet.

"Trudy, my sweet, the truck is moving. It's on its way to the gas station. . . . Pretend orange juice is gas," Sally said as they made their way to the table.

"I must put on my makeup," Sally announced as soon as Trudy was settled. There was really only room for three at the kitchen table, but she didn't like to acknowledge that fact. "Daddy, will you cut Trudy's pancake while she gasses up?"

In the next fifteen minutes, all the details got organized somehow, the lunchboxes packed and in the right hands, everyone combed with his own comb, and all the right jackets and hats on the right bodies and heads. Paul would take Paulie to P.S. 41 while she dropped off Trudy at nursery school. As they stepped out on the sidewalk, the cold wind whirled trash and grit around them.

"If the computer is down, I'll be home late," Paul said.

"But do call! Good luck on your cat-hunting —" she cried as Paul and Paulie walked away with identical, slightly pigeon-toed strides. The only difference was that Paulie's shoelaces were untied.

At 5:30 when Sally returned, the small apartment was bizarrely quiet. "Shhh!" Paulie and Trudy were crouched on the living room carpet staring at the sofa, while Connie read a paperback in the gold chair.

"The name is Topaze," Paulie cried. "She's white with blue eyes. Three years old, likes children, hates dogs."

"And I got a white cat called Fluffy," Trudy added. "She's Topaze's sister."

While Sally shot an anguished look at Connie, Trudy continued, "Fluffy is magically invisible."

"As soon as we opened the box, Topaze ran behind the sofa. She's been there for hours," Paulie complained. "And Trudy keeps making loud noises."

"I do not," shrieked Trudy.

"Just let her get used to you," Connie advised good-naturedly, beginning to put on her duffle coat. She had a son waiting for her in Brooklyn whom somebody else was watching. "It was fifteen dollars, and the cab cost five dollars, so there's no change."

"That's fine. It was extremely nice of you to help Paulie. See you tomorrow."

"And your husband called at five and said the computer broke down on schedule."

As soon as Connie left, Sally kicked off her high heels and sat down on the rug with her arm around Paulie's shoulder. "Were there lots of other cats?"

"Oh, hundreds."

"Why did you pick Topaze?"

Paulie's blue eyes were indignant. "Mommy, she was *lying* in her litter. She looked so depressed I wanted to rescue her. She has sad eyes."

Oh my, Sally thought. What a reason! "Did Connie say she was healthy?"

"Oh, super-healthy. She was just de-wormed."

Later, while Trudy was singing in the bathtub, Topaze slipped out from her hiding place. Head held high, she began nibbling the foliage of Sally's favorite plant. Topaze was a sleek, well-grown, powerful animal, not at all dainty and ladylike as Sally had imagined. When she turned her face, Sally thought she saw something like wild anguish in her blue eyes. Then Topaze began sinking her sharp claws into the carpet.

Paulie ran to get the catfood. "Here, Topaze, Topaze. I'm going to call her Topaze. I like it better than Minnie."

"Honey, I'm not sure, but I think that dieffenbachia she was chewing is a poisonous plant. Another name is Dumb Cane or Mother-in-Law's Tongue because, I think, it can poison you."

Trudy rushed into the living room plump and rosy from her bath. "Let's see my cat's sister."

"Honey, get a towel. You're all wet. You're staining the floor."

"Shouldn't we throw away the plant?" Paulie said.

"Throw away the plant! Paulie, my beautiful plant!"

"Well, she's eating it again. I don't want my cat to die."

"Move her away."

"I'm afraid. Her claws are so long!"

Sally's heart was shrinking in response to these powerful conflicting demands. Also she was hungry; it had been a miserable day at work; she had a feeling she was going to be fired from her publishing job, and they would never have the money to move from this tiny apartment with its poisonous plants.

"Connie would have mentioned plant-eating if it was dangerous."

Sally soothed Paulie, as she embraced the squirming Trudy with a bath towel. "Let's just have our dinner and be calm. Maybe Daddy can hang the dieffenbachia from the ceiling."

"She'll be dead by then."

"Oh quit it, Paulie."

By the time the excited children had finally fallen asleep, Topaze had stopped eating foliage and had gobbled up the tablespoon of catfood in the plastic bowl and used the plastic litter box in a thoroughly civilized way. But despite his careful Indian-footed approach, when Paul let himself in the door, Topaze took fright and rushed back under the sofa.

"How are you?" Sally asked.

"Tired."

"Do you want to eat?"

"I'm too tired. But I guess I ought to eat something. Do you have any cake?"

"No."

All unaware, Paul threw himself down on the sofa.

"There is a highly frightened cat cowering underneath you."

"I'm not such a dangerous fellow, am I?" Paul said, throwing his head back against the pillows, quite pleased with the idea.

Anyone looking at Paul could see that he was not a dangerous fellow. As a boy he had been poor in sports and had liked chess, geography, and playing the violin. Although this kind of shy, melancholy boy passes a dull childhood and a miserable adolescence, he often grows up to be highly attractive to women. Sally was considered lucky to have snared Paul when they were still in college, and Paul had grown more attractive each year, though he was still melancholy for a number of reasons. He didn't like his job, which he considered a dead end, or living in a city. He disliked his children's noisiness and being waked in the middle of the night by their nightmares and stomachaches. He felt he had reached thirty without accomplishing anything.

In a moment, Topaze poked her head out and paraded past the sofa. "A good-looking cat. Paulie has good taste." When Topaze leaped up on the cushion right next to Paul, he smiled. "You see? I'm harmless and well loved by animals."

"Paulie will be jealous. He's afraid to go near her. I'm afraid he has poor taste if he was looking for a cuddly animal," Sally said. "Topaze seems to think a lot of herself. She does just what she likes."

Paul stroked Topaze with his long white hands, and she began to purr. "Look how she goes for it. . . . "

The sight of Topaze—whom she had put down as snooty—helplessly turning her neck and belly up to Paul after a moment's acquaintance vaguely disturbed Sally.

"She really goes for it. . . . "

"Are you sure you don't want dinner?"

"No. I'm much too tired. Too tired even to read. I think I'll go to sleep." But he kept on rhythmically stroking Topaze.

Sally went into the bedroom to put on her nightgown. All of a sudden she, too, felt unusually tired. Why had she allowed Paulie to hold her to the promise of the red-circled day on the calendar? A Thursday, of all days. It was too exhausting to acquire a cat in the middle of the week. As she walked back around the jutting edge of the double bed that took up most of the minuscule bedroom, Sally violently banged her thigh, certainly for the millionth time. "Ow," she cried to herself in pain and frustration. "Ow."

Given their cramped surroundings, it was not peculiar that Sally, sitting on her bed, still rubbing her leg from her collision, should hear loud crashing in the hallway from another accident. Paul struggled into the bedroom cursing, with Trudy's wooden rocking horse in his hands. He looked dangerous, as though he might break the rocking horse over Sally's head.

"When the hell are you going to get rid of this thing?" he demanded.

"Well, she's still using it, Paul," Sally said mildly. They had had this conversation several times before. "As soon as she stops using it, I'll get rid of it."

"Why can't she put it away? Why do we have to have a death trap in the hallway?"

"It's my fault, Paul. I forgot to put it back in the closet. We were excited about the cat, and I didn't get to pick up, and anyway I was tired."

Usually remarking that she was tired was enough to silence Paul, but tonight he went on. "Why does she need a rocking horse anyway? Millions of children grow to maturity without having a rocking horse. I never had a rocking horse."

"She likes to rock. Rocking is important for little children. Why are you making such a fuss?"

"I can't stand this place," he replied simply. "This place is a disaster. Everywhere you walk there are goddamn toys under your feet. I'm going to throw them all in the incinerator. The next one I find goes straight down the incinerator."

Paul had complained about the children's toys before, but never in this tone of virulent hatred. He banged the rocking horse down in the corner.

"The goddamn cat litter box is right next to the toilet. How can I pee with a goddamn litter box in my face?"

"The bathroom is small, Paulie." Sally had the unfortunate habit of getting her son's and her husband's names mixed up at tense moments like this. "But where else can we put it? When you agreed to a cat, you knew it would have a litter box," she continued in a bland, reasonable tone.

"When I agreed to a cat . . . when I agreed to a cat . . ." Paul's face turned evil and red. "I didn't agree to any of this menagerie. It was all foisted on me. . . ."

"Uhn." Sally gave a gulp as though she had been hit in the stomach and drew up her feet on the bed. She felt like a boxer who'd been whacked into the ropes.

"I've been miserable for years now," Paul continued in a loud, strained voice. "For years. Since Paulie. You accuse me of making a fuss. You're the one who's always fussing. You're always worrying. Why must you always be goddamn worrying?"

Sally's voice came out muffled and remote. Paul had never attacked her in this way before, had never displayed such contempt. In her surprise and distress she felt as if she were having somebody else's argument.

"With children you have to worry."

"You don't worry about me!"

"Of course I do. Besides, you're a grown-up."

Paul began pacing up and down in the narrow space between the bed and the bureau. "We never go anywhere. We never do anything. First it was a diaper pail, and now it's a litter box. If I had my way, I'd be out of here in ten minutes. I'd pack my socks and go to the bus station."

By now Sally had sunk way down in the bed and had pulled the comforter up to her nose; she seemed a strange, mouthless figure.

"You don't even answer me." Paul stared at her in fury. His contorted face made him look like a different man. She pulled away the coverlet from her face but remained silent, tears rolling from her eyes.

"You don't even answer me."

"I am too upset to say anything." He could see it was true. She looked like a different woman.

Suddenly a whitish blur slipped by, leaping on Sally's side of the bed. They jumped. It was Topaze, mewing pitifully.

"Oh Lord, it must still be hungry. Why should I be the one to feed it? I have enough mouths to feed." Sally turned toward Paul. "Paul, you do it."

Muttering "This place is a pesthole," Paul went into the kitchen and turned on the light. Sally turned out her bedside light. When he returned, smelling a little of fish, there was only a narrow ribbon of light falling on his pillow.

"What shall we do then?" Sally asked miserably.

"I don't know. Go to sleep," he replied.

Paul turned out his light. Within a few minutes they heard sinister rustlings and scratchings in the living room.

Sally got out of bed. "I'm going to close the bedroom door. The children are old enough to be by themselves. I don't want that animal walking over me while I'm asleep." She turned suddenly and shouted into the darkness, "I've been walked on enough!"

"Good idea."

Sally shut the door. Paul was curled up catlike on his side of the bed facing the wall, one slender leg crossed over the other. Soon they heard violent scratching on the door of the bedroom. Sally got up and went to their bathroom, opened up the medicine cabinet looking for a Valium. When she crawled back in bed, Paul sat up and silently reached over to give her a good-night kiss. She lifted her face.

"There's nothing we can do," she said. "Unless you want to leave."

"Just go to sleep."

They slept. Although Topaze wandered nocturnally, stepping near the face of the three-year-old, picking her way among the prickly cactus pots on the windowsill, sniffing at the ancient roach powder between the refrigerator and the wall, that night she came to no harm.

44-28

Lois is forty-four, the mother of two adolescent children, divorced, a law professor at N.Y.U. On Friday she is going to London for six months to do research, and she has only four days to pack, send her children off to camp, find a reliable tenant for her house, and say good-bye to her young lover, whom she doesn't expect to take up with again when she comes home.

Lois originally chose this lover because he was married and unsuitable; now she has fallen in love with him and is angry at herself and him. She wants to be free so that she can find a new man she may not love as much, who will be her helpmeet for the rest of her life. These are the words she is thinking of using in saying farewell to her lover, but she is already smiling at the expression she imagines she will see on his clever, sarcastic face when she says "helpmeet." She is trying to think of a substitute word as she absently carries cardboard boxes up to the second floor. The lover is coming over soon to help her with this heavy work.

Lois is always nervous about having her friends meet Charles because, at the expensive private school her son attends, he is the gym instructor. There is something about his being a gym instructor that she dislikes even more than his being married or being young. Of course, he is in very good shape and very well muscled, but she feels he is an underachiever. Charles could have been a lawyer if he had tried or a philosophy instructor—anything that would make her feel less like a chaser of athletic young men. Indeed, it was the sight of him in white tennis shorts that first drew her attention—also his antic humor. She remembers how he approached her while she was walking her dog on Thirteenth Street and said soberly, "Mrs. Richman, may I stroll with you in the gutters of Gotham?"

Charles has offered to board her dog while she is in London. It would be unfair to the dog to kennel her solely to avoid seeing Charles again when she returns. She hasn't made up her mind yet. Perhaps she will get rid of the dog, too, while she is in a purifying state of mind. The two children she cannot get rid of, though the thought has crossed her mind once or twice. Lois's daughter is sixteen and will be going to Vassar in the fall. She will visit her father at Christmastime. Her son is only twelve and will go to school for one term in London. A chess player and model-constructor, he may not even notice that he is in London. He has been in a dreamworld ever since his father moved to California a year ago. He hasn't even thought it odd that Charles drops by so frequently. Perhaps she should just give the dog to Charles. Lois bought Geraldine for comfort in the early days of her divorce, so it would be a double betrayal to palm them off on each other.

What she really wants is for Charles to leave his wife and come and live with her, but she doesn't know it yet. She prefers to divest herself of everything rather than entertain the idea. Charles is twenty-eight years old. Many times she has gone over in her head the following figure combinations: 44-28, 54-38, 64-48, 74-58, just as when she was longing to get pregnant she kept imagining May-January, June-February, July-March.

While Lois is at the very back of a walk-in closet, sorting out her son's clothes in piles for camp, for London, for storage, she hears the doorbell ring. At the door she finds a very well dressed woman, about twenty-eight, in extremely good repair, with a deep, even tan. She is wearing a pair of buff silk overalls. Her hair, bouncing in glossy, blond-tipped curls around her face, has recently been blow-dried by a master hand.

"The rental agent sent me over. I'm Marabel Bush." She has a strong Southern accent.

"Hello," says Lois in a noncommittal way. "Are you a family or part of a group?"

"We're a couple. My husband's firm sent him to New York, and I just hated to stay home all by myself."

"Why do you need a three-story house, if I may ask?"

"Well, we do heaps of entertaining, and my grandmother and my husband's daddy will be visiting."

Lois doesn't absolutely need the rental money for the house.

She has been so fussy about prospective tenants that the agent has given up tagging along. "Well, come in and take a look," she says dubiously.

As Lois follows Mrs. Bush up the narrow stairs of the brownstone, she grows conscious of her own dowdy appearance. She's wearing jeans and a saggy velour poncho that she used long ago as a beach dress. Her long, unwashed brown hair hangs down, while her gray hairs reach for the sky. She has previously decided to look as terrible as possible when she tells Charles that she is quitting their affair. Now, staring at trim Mrs. Bush in her trim silk overalls, she thinks she may have gone too far in dishevelment.

Mrs. Bush is by no means gushing about the layout and decor of Lois's brownstone. Admittedly, the rooms are quite small, the furniture on the plain side. Lois bought the house with a legacy her father left her, over the protests of her former husband. Now it has doubled in value, giving Lois much satisfaction. She pats the mahogany bannister lovingly as they ascend to the bedroom floor. The doors to the children's rooms are closed, and she opens them just half a crack. "We haven't cleaned these smaller bedrooms yet, but we're planning to tomorrow."

"We'll take it," says Mrs. Bush unexpectedly, without any preamble. "It's so old-fashioned. Granny will love it."

Lois is not eager to rent to Marabel Bush. Lois is envious of Marabel's looks and manicure and thinks she will have wild parties despite Granny's restraining influence, but Lois has forgotten to put in any of the escape hatches she devised when showing the house to other people.

"Oil bills and electricity are all extra, of course," she says, "and you must pay the man who mows and weeds the garden."

"Certainly," says Mrs. Bush in velvety tones.

"We'll need two months' security as well."

Mrs. Bush opens her mail-pouch handbag and removes her texturized checkbook with its retractable silver-plated pen.

"No noisy parties," Lois continues. "I must stay on good

terms with my neighbors. They've been kind to me. Also, I'll be in London, and I won't be able to help you if any emergencies arise. But I'll leave a list of plumbers, electricians, and such, because things do break down in an old house."

Just then the doorbell rings, and Charles comes bounding up the steps. Even in his housecleaning rags he looks radiant. Lately he's been eating no meat and running an hour a day before breakfast, and this has given him a pared-down look of pure energy. He has a long Scandinavian head, blond hair cut too short, green eyes, a glossy brown mustache. (If only he didn't make such monkey faces, twisting up his mouth in mock disdain or boredom.) At sight of this robust, wonderful-looking man, some devil takes hold of Lois, who is normally so circumspect. "Mrs. Bush, I'd like you to meet my husband, Charles. Charles, our new tenant, Mrs. Bush."

Charles's eyes bulge in surprise, but he quickly bolts his face down in a casual smile.

"Charles was only fourteen when we married," Lois continues. "Our son is twelve."

Mrs. Bush stares in amazement. After a moment or two of inertia, she puts her checkbook back in her purse without writing a check, then quickly makes off, back to the rental agent to look at the terms of the lease.

"What were you doing there, Lo?" Charles asks when Lois reappears from downstairs. "What was that for?"

"Oh, Charles . . ." Lois rakes her fingers through her hair. "I don't know what I'm doing. I feel so harried."

As soon as Lois says this, she really feels harried for the first time. "I didn't like that dame. She'll be sleeping in my bed, and I wanted to shake her up."

"Cute number." Charles makes his sex-fiend face by rolling his eyes and smacking his lips. "But no bosom." Lois would normally be flattered by this remark, would bask in it, but today she is irritated. She imagines Charles in her bed making love to Mrs. Bush. "Also, she looks as though she spends her entire day in front of the mirror getting dressed," Charles says.

"Stop," replies Lois shrilly. "You know she looks great!"

Her soon-to-be-abandoned lover could not be behaving more nicely, but Lois is growing more angry. It would have comforted her to know that Charles's wife, a twenty-five-year-old receptionist, spends long hours every day getting dressed in front of the mirror, that Charles's wife has a bosom like an ironing board, a disposition like an ironing board. They have never discussed Charles's marital situation. He has never stayed all night. He usually says, "Back to Wuthering Heights," or, "It's been a pleasure visiting you, Miss Scarlett," before he climbs into his burnt-sienna briefs and tiptoes away. Charles can never be playful in this particular way with his wife, Barbara, but Lois doesn't know that.

The two of them begin stacking cartons for storage, but before long the rental agent telephones. Mrs. Bush has changed her mind; she prefers Westchester after all. At this news Charles begins to smile. While Lois is saying, "Oh, well, so we won't have a tenant; it really doesn't matter," he is grinning cheerfully.

"You know, Lois, I was going to suggest that if you didn't find anyone, *we* could live in the house for you."

"Are you joking?"

"Well, you know I can't pay your kind of rent. But I could take care of your garden and baby-sit Geraldine. She'd be happier here than in a three-room apartment, and so would I."

"You and Geraldine and *Barbara*?"

"Is that so outlandish?"

Lois is so furious at this hateful suggestion that her whole body trembles. "Yes, it is! Most outlandish! You crass—ballplayer!"

Charles could willingly clobber Lois, but he exercises self-control. His strong legs propel him around the room several times in great agitation.

"Lois, I'm sorry I suggested it, since it's made you unhappy," he says finally. "If I could unsay it, I would, if you would unsay the 'ballplayer' bit. That was really low."

"It's quite an appropriate epithet," Lois replies in her loftiest, most cutting tones. "Am I a pinch hitter or not?"

Charles stops and stares at Lois in astonishment. Charles indeed loves Lois, but as an earth mother who will take care of his needs without asking anything for herself. As a matter of fact, that is precisely how Lois has always behaved. Until this moment, she has enjoyed being an earth mother.

"I wish I knew why you feel so offended," Charles says.

"Oh, just get the hell out! Go be ironic someplace else."

"Well, call me. When you want me to take Geraldine, just give me a call."

Throughout the tumult preceding her divorce, Lois never once acted badly. She never gave her husband the satisfaction of a single unjustified insult—not even when he moved out, leaving her to tell the bad news to the children. Her anger took the form of drinking too much and throwing away his mail. Now she screams, "Get the hell out!" and aims a child's sneaker at Charles. It hits him in the shoulder. Charles leaves the room with exaggerated slowness. He is too hurt to think of a clever exit line.

Lois flings herself down on a pile of winter clothes. "Don't go, Charles," she says in a tiny voice as soon as she hears the downstairs door slam. She begins to cry in the shattering way she used to when she was twelve. She forgets that she planned to abandon Charles, that she has abandoned him. He will never seem more desirable than he does now, when she knows she will not see him again.

To Forget August

On Sunday morning two mid-thirtyish neighbors stand together at the boundary of their contiguous backyards in Chelsea. She has been weeding her garden when he suddenly appears at the straggling ilex that divides their property, searching for a trowel. When she produces one, he asks if she is busy. She says yes she is, the children are away for a couple of hours, it's her big opportunity to get things done. Nevertheless she steps through the ilex, pulls up a rickety garden chair, and sits down in August Muhlenberg's backyard.

Leila has always been curious about this wonderful-looking man who is never called Augie or Gus, but for reasons she doesn't understand their conversation is always a sparring match. Because he is a writer, he makes her nervous. His wasteful habits puzzle her. Alone in a house as big as her own, he leaves lights burning all night. He gardens sporadically, planting and then neglecting. On frigid winter days he keeps windows open. At this unexpected contact Leila feels desperate to utter something approaching normal speech, but she is unable to think of a single word. He doesn't help her.

"I've never seen you bareheaded before," she remarks at last, delighted by the thick, silky, prematurely white head of hair he has revealed. "Where is your battered Irish hat?"

"Surely we have something better to talk about than hats," he replies.

"I'm not certain we do."

They sit in uncomfortable silence. Over a period of six years, ever since her younger son was born and she moved into this brownstone, she and August have had hundreds of conversations, but always in passing, she in her backyard, he in his. Because they live on different streets, they rarely run into each other. On the sidewalk he has a sullen remote look not apparent in the backyard, his face guarded by his down-drooping hat. Does he even know that her husband has moved away? Leila has a sudden happy idea.

"Since you've interrupted my free morning, August, why don't you amuse me with a story?"

"Gladly."

"About a woman."

"To be sure." He rubs his thick dappled brown and gray beard. "Hmm. A woman." Without taking another moment's thought, he begins in a booming voice.

"Once there was a woman who did not usually drink. One day she was faced with the housework which she had somehow let slip. Depressed in advance, she poured some gin which she happened to have in the cupboard into some orange juice and drank it. Encouraged by the mellow feeling which made cleaning the inside of the refrigerator and scrubbing down the kitchen woodwork tolerable, she fixed herself an even longer, stronger drink and commenced to wash the kitchen floor. Along about then her three-year-old daughter, Lorelei, came in from playing, and wanting to get her off the kitchen floor, the woman thought of putting her in the bathtub."

Here August gives a deep, melodramatic sigh. "Must I continue? The end of my story is painful. A third gin and orange enabled the woman to finish the job in record time with a high degree of cleanliness, but when she recollected the little girl in the bathtub, it was far too late." August regards her with a wicked glint in his eye. "Well, how do you like it? I'll call it 'Too Late for Lorelei.'"

Leila is disappointed in August. "Why are you telling me this terrible story? Are you trying to scare me or make me feel guilty? Small children play in the bathtub for hours without coming to harm. If it's morality you want, wouldn't it be better if the woman is punished for sex? With the delivery boy perhaps?"

August looks ruffled. "You misunderstand me. I was illustrating the tyranny of housecleaning, a completely different moral. I've never noticed any desire to houseclean in you, so I don't see why you're taking all this personally."

"I am a mother, therefore I houseclean. And I've been known to take a drink in the afternoon. As a matter of fact, when my husband first left, I drank quite a bit."

August grins disarmingly. "Do you *have* any gin, by the way? It was thirst that drove me in this direction."

"You are a fraud." Leila begins to laugh. "I have rum in the cupboard. I think I have a little Drambuie."

"Let's drink together until your children come home. How else to spend a sunny Sunday?"

Leila rises to go back to her house but stops, hesitating. "Whatever made you pick drowning? I'd really like to know. Was it fear of impending drunkenness?"

"Right, totally right. Also, I just lost my favorite hat and am feeling anguish over it, so my story was revenge for your noticing. A very hostile story, I must admit."

Leila is dazzled by August's rude honesty or honest rudeness. Also, his feelings are easily hurt—just like hers. "I'm glad we're getting to know each other so well. Rum in orange juice for you?"

"Yes, but before we drink, why don't we kiss and make up?"

At the time it seems clear to Leila that August is literally offering to kiss her. Later on, she is not so sure. In any case, she remarks hesitantly, "If we kissed, all the tenants in the high rise would notice."

August rises and slowly moves toward her, palms open, as if approaching a dangerous sociopath. "Don't be self-conscious. Just a friendly kiss between neighbors."

They embrace. Although Leila is tall and thin and August is middle-sized and hefty, they seem custom-made for this particular embrace. For one moment she thinks, Why am I getting involved with this brilliant nut, just the sort I always fall for? Then she forgets her powerful insight.

The couple are devoted lovers all summer. August buys a more lighthearted cap. He stops working on his book and begins taking her two sons to Yankee games. They all go to Philadelphia to see the Liberty Bell and walk through a model of the human heart in the Franklin Institute.

His self-absorption, elusiveness, and nasty remarks at her expense are balanced out by his charm, funny stories, and sincere regard for her children. Her suspiciousness, tendency to worry, and curiosity about his inner life are balanced out by her exquisite tact and rapid achievement of mature sexual pleasure.

By fall they are talking of selling one house and living together in greatly increased luxury in the other. Yet cracks are noted in his good humor because, though he has stopped suffering from insomnia, bad dreams, drunkenness, and impulsive behavior, August has also stopped writing.

One evening as they are coming out of the local movie house he says, "I have a contract for this book, as you know, and if I don't finish I will be in big trouble. I've been blocked before, but it was always misery, and this is so painless that I'm scared it's serious. Permanent even."

"How can I help?"

"Let me go to London until January. I'll come back to you with a book and cashmere sweaters for everyone."

She agrees, but August does not return. He meets a woman and is in North Africa by Christmastime.

To fall out of love one must remove oneself from the object of desire. This technique worked wonderfully for August, but Leila is having a much harder time. She thinks more about August than she ever does about her ex-husband.

After August's long, enigmatic letter postponing their life together until he is "ready to appreciate her excellence," Leila causes a stockaded fence to be built between their properties, replacing the ilexes. Only good advice and a local ordinance keep her from adding barbed wire to the top of the fence.

His book appears speedily the following fall and receives wonderful reviews. To her irritation she notices that it is dedi-

cated to her children. By then they have stopped mentioning
August. While she is meditating further revenge, the house on
the next street is either sold or rented out to strangers. Her
fence turns out a horrible mistake, for she has lost a good view
of the people living in August's place, nor can she easily eaves-
drop to find out if he is coming back. She haunts her garden,
spending tedious hours planting bulbs in undesirable loca-
tions, but the only clue she discovers is the occasional scent of
a garlicky dinner or the inadvertent blast of a stereophonic
quartet. How long will August stay away? As a sign of fury, she
hangs wet laundry over the fence, but there is no response.

A Rent-Stabilized Romance

Beryl and Peter hoped to get married. For more than two years they had been sharing lives without actually sharing the same apartment. Beryl had a tiny, rent-stabilized studio with a view of the Hudson which she'd occupied ever since she had come to New York after college. She noticed that newcomers to town sometimes treated her spitefully when she spoke of her apartment, so she avoided mentioning the fantastically low rent. Peter lived in a cheap third-floor walk-up in a Lower East Side tenement without a lock on the downstairs front door, an unsuitable place for a nervous bride. While Beryl believed it just a matter of time before she met a violent end at the hands of muggers, Peter was able to stroll serenely through his terrifying neighborhood.

In time as most of their friends changed partners or married, their own relationship seemed slightly pallid. "You mean you don't live together?" people were always remarking. Beryl and Peter grew tired of pointing out that their combined rents could not buy them a decent dwelling in Manhattan. Still, they lived well for a librarian and a college textbook editor, because they spent the money they saved on rent for luxuries like restaurant meals and theater tickets. They felt they lived a sophisticated, lively life.

"Would you really want to move to New Jersey and have to get up early in the morning?" Beryl asked Peter. "And have to leave the opera before the last act?" "No way," Peter replied.

"But wouldn't it be nice to spend all our free time together?" Peter asked Beryl. "Heavenly," Beryl answered. "But exactly how are we going to manage it?"

One Wednesday night after enjoying an Indian meal and a movie on W. 13th Street, Peter urgently persuaded Beryl to his apartment. At about 10:30 he awakened to find Beryl breathing into his ear. "I have to go home now," she was whispering.

"Aw, Beryl, sweetie, stay the night."

"Just take me as far as the crosstown bus. I need some books for work tomorrow."

Later, standing on a street corner in a distant neighborhood in which Beryl had some confidence, Peter felt lonely and manipulated as he waved her off on the bus. Her heart-shaped face, which he normally thought of as heartbreaking and lovely, seemed a pale gloating triangle in the bus window. "If she loved me, she'd get rid of that damned studio," he thought.

Saturday night Peter stayed over at Beryl's. In the morning, the place reminded Peter of a dollhouse. He couldn't bear to see Beryl dishing up breakfast at her doll-sized stove, breaking eggs into a tiny frying pan. The wooden dish rack she unfolded before washing the dishes enraged him. Beryl's bed, small enough to fit into the ingenious alcove she'd devised, had suddenly grown too short for his tall, narrow frame. His back ached; his feet itched. The reading lamps were hung at the wrong height. Peter crashed around the place all Sunday morning, then left on a nonexistent errand downtown.

To make up for disloyal thoughts, on the following Tuesday after work Peter cooked a corned beef and cabbage dinner for Beryl in his old-fashioned kitchen. After dinner they lay comfortably in the front room of the railroad flat on Peter's plump sofa pillows reading *Anna Karenina* out loud. When they stopped at chapter six, put on their raincoats and went outside, they found a bum lounging on Peter's front steps in a cold November drizzle. As they gingerly went past, the bum grabbed Peter's ankle with both filthy hands. Peter just said, "Let go, man," and shook his leg, and the man let go and slumped to the side. But Beryl felt dizzy after the incident, and they had to drop their plans to go out for Irish coffee.

As they boarded the 102 Uptown bus, Beryl was having disloyal thoughts of her own. Peter was thoughtful, charming, well read, and had a secure position as a librarian, but was he really a reliable person to marry? Wasn't he sort of outside society? He cared nothing for appearances—living in that dump.

He always looked rumpled because he let his drip-dry shirts tumble around for hours while he read a book. He never called his mother and father in Schenectady. He had never opened an Individual Retirement Account.

Beryl began sleeping poorly. She dreamed about drowning in chocolate pudding, also about having one of her arms eaten by rats while the doorman of her apartment building looked on. Just at this time, Beryl was suffering a bad period at work. She'd earned a promotion, but instead of inspiring joy the change was causing panic. Her new boss, a Dr. Jekyll, was considerate one minute, vicious the next. The new secretary, Manuel, was impossible. They could not get along together, she complained to Peter. He was much less efficient than her old secretary. Besides, he seemed to hate her.

"In the morning I can barely exchange greetings with him. We don't say good morning. I look at him blankly and say, 'Manuel,' and he looks at me in a funny way and lisps, 'Beryl.'"

"You can't lisp 'Beryl.' There are no *s*'s," Peter objected.

"You know what I mean. He says it in an insinuating way. He makes it sound horrible. He insinuates and he peeks at me from under his bleached blond bangs. How am I going to deal with him?"

"Why don't you take him to lunch and show him you appreciate him?"

"Peter, you're not listening. I don't appreciate him. I hate him. He's so alien."

"Every other person in New York is alien. You know it, honey. He's only been working for you for two weeks. Maybe you'll get used to each other."

"Your optimism is not helpful."

"I'm sorry."

At the same time, Peter's job prospects were bleak. The only attractive opening at the N.Y.U. library in the last two years had gone to a woman whom Peter considered a birdbrain. His supervisor was deaf to complaint, written or verbal. When Peter complained to Beryl, all she could think of to say was, "Maybe you could work at Columbia."

Soon Peter and Beryl began feeling tired simultaneously. They didn't have the strength to stand on line to see a good movie. They let their ballet subscription lapse. They just felt like going home and sleeping.

One afternoon before Thanksgiving, Peter telephoned Beryl at work. She didn't recognize his voice at first because it sounded so warm and animated.

"I think I've found the way to be together," he said. "My friend Lou has a brother in town from Europe. He's been hiring English teachers for an American high school in Germany. We could do that, Beryl. You have Ed. credits and so have I."

Beryl felt shaken. "What are you talking about?"

"We could get married next month—move to Germany for two years. Support ourselves—have fun. The term starts in February."

"What about our jobs?"

"What *about* our jobs? We can get other jobs later on if we want to move back here. Do you really like your work? What about your boss? What about horrible Manuel? The only thing is, the brother—Jack Berner—is leaving for Boston tomorrow. He wants to hire two more teachers before he flies back on Sunday. If we want to meet him, we have to do it tonight. Can you come to East 6th Street at seven o'clock?"

"Oh, Peter, you know I hate that neighborhood!"

"It's just for once. I'll have to meet you there because I'm working late tonight." His voice grew portentous. "We're in a big trap here, Beryl, and this is a chance to get out."

"I don't know. I'm not ready for a big change like that. I'm a conservative person. Maybe my apartment will go co-op soon, and then I can sell out and leave."

Peter was exasperated. "Beryl, it's not as if I'm asking you to go to Tanzania and live with tsetse flies or go prospecting in

Alaska. This is Western Europe. Think of the great vacations we can take—the operas and ballets—sitting in cafés—Italy in winter—Paris at Christmas—the Orient Express—our own apartment!"

"What about terrorists?"

Peter's voice took on a muffled, dead note. "Beryl, just come to this address tonight, OK? You don't have to commit yourself to anything. Just meet the guy. Trust me a little. I promise I won't go if it sounds chancy. But I feel excited! I know we can manage. I'm ready for it!"

That evening Beryl was late coming to meet Jack Berner. She waited at her office a little too long because she didn't want to turn up before Peter, and then the bus ride downtown took far longer than she had expected. Beryl felt too fearful to take the speedier subway. Even if she weren't unnerved by the threat of danger and confused by the noise and filth, she was depressed by the sad-looking people heading for unimaginable lives in Brooklyn. Seated on the east side of the brightly lit bus, squashed by the standees hanging over her shoulder batting her with packages, she kept peering out the window through the darkness, looking for signposts.

Beryl got off at the right stop at last and quickly crossed the street, trying not to feel anxious. She wished she had had her running shoes with her at work so she did not have to totter along on her high heels. Would she be able to run at all if she were attacked? First came a brightly lighted bodega with teenagers hanging around outside, which she passed in a hurry without looking left or right, then a long dark stretch of sidewalk roofed with a wooden scaffolding. A dumpster and a pile of cinder blocks forced her briefly into the gutter. No one at all was around in the blackness, and she still had another long block to go.

Somehow some tiny pebbles from a sandpile at the curb had penetrated her shoe. She shook her foot once or twice but couldn't dislodge the stones. She was rushing along twice as fast as usual, despite a grinding pain in her toe, when she caught sight of a man's figure ahead of her. If she continued at her present pace, she would soon catch up with him. She decided against hurrying: (1) As long as the stranger was ahead of her, he could have no thoughts of harming her. (2) She could call on him for aid, perhaps, if she were attacked.

So they continued along in this shadowy fashion for a block until they came to a wide, well-lit intersection. The man paused for the red light, and Beryl stood on one foot about ten paces behind, studying his back. She felt safer here. He was tall and narrow with fragile hunched shoulders, perhaps a touch of scoliosis. With amusement Beryl realized that her fantasies about this fellow as attacker or rescuer were absurd. He had no more violence in him than did a blade of grass.

She determined to hurry past him then to reach shelter sooner. As she drew near enough to see him well under the bright streetlamp, she stopped, exhausted and depressed. She thought with longing of her cozy alcove with a cup of hot cocoa on the bedside table. She saw herself mounting the dizzying steps to a 747 with a thin unstable man with hunched shoulders. In the clarifying light, the man on the corner was her fiancé, Peter.

Surfaces

Roger and Penny live in Barlow House, a prizewinning co-op apartment house on 10th Street. Because the facade of Barlow House is drab brown stone, the visitor stepping past the soberly clad doorman is amazed to find himself in the middle of a tropical rain forest. Among the humid, immaculately kept beds of jungle foliage stands a tall, elegant cage containing a gentle capuchin monkey. The jungle stream plashes, the foliage writhes, the monkey frolics. Waiting for tardy friends and relations in the lobby of Barlow House is never a bore.

Roger met Penny just after his divorce, at a Christmas party given by his boss's wife, a party marking his reentry into the cold social world as a single man. Most of the partygoers were Wall Street people, but their hostess had recently taken up the dance, so a portion of the guest list came from her studio. Suddenly the oak-paneled elevator doors opened, and over the oriental carpet rushed a pack of young dancers in such remarkable physical shape that they made the middle-aged guests in their concealing finery feel sick. The girls with their neat flexible waists, the young men with their long muscular legs and long hair or shaven heads, arrogantly speaking only to each other, exclaiming loudly over the Yule log burning in the grate, devouring the chicken mousse and the eggnog and brandy and pfeffernuss as if calories did not exist, they generally acted, as one guest put it, as if they had never been let out before.

Among the dark girls in handknit shawls and mirrored smocks, girls named Masha and Natalya, was one who resembled Alice in Wonderland. A fair-haired girl with dark, well-marked eyebrows over a long straight nose, she wore a blue gingham frock with a white organdy apron and black slippers with delicate straps across the instep. A beauty, although one of her front teeth was slightly chipped. She hung back from the others, examining the cakes and carafes on the buffet as if they said, "Eat me," "Drink me."

Roger, standing across the room discussing the bond issue

of the moment, took one look, overcame thirty-five years of conservative behavior, and rushed to her side.

How lucky he was! When she opened her delicately modeled lips, her conversation was shy but intelligent. She was not seventeen, as he had feared, but twenty-two. Her father dead in Vietnam, her mother removed to Houston, she lived with several other dancers in a ramshackle apartment on Second Avenue.

As Roger discovered when he took her home with him that evening, she was not inexperienced with men. Poor orphan, seduced by an aging ballet master, a Eurasian flutist, and a seventeen-year-old corps boy, until Roger she had not found a single man to care for her.

Of course, Roger's colleagues mocked his speedy elopement three weeks later, but only behind his back. No one seeing the couple at their wedding party could help being touched by their mutual devotion. Roger called Penny "my bag of gold." Penny had no pet name for Roger, but she instinctively turned toward him no matter what part of the room he moved in, as if by tropism.

Lucky Roger had bought several co-op apartments as investments. The very week of their elopement a splendid apartment fell vacant, and Penny was installed as a new bride in Barlow House. Although Penny gave up dancing professionally, by ingenious arrangement the spare bedroom was converted to a mirrored studio with barre where she could practice daily to preserve her stretch. She devoted the rest of her time to decorating, spending hours on a tall ladder stapling floral Liberty fabric to the walls and ceilings.

When the decorating phase was over, Penny felt letdown and lonely. Her friends in the company were all on the road now, and they were jealous of her good fortune, in any case. She came to realize that Masha and Natalya had never been sincere.

Now Penny bought dance subscriptions, many of them. Almost every night she dressed up and they went out. She enjoyed sitting in the First Ring of the New York State Theater. They would drink champagne among crowds on the Promenade at intermissions, then hurry to their seats as the last warning bell rang. "We're late," she would cry, and Roger would smile. Because the seats were on the aisle, she could dash in through a dark luxurious tunnel, dropping as though from a chute into E101. Remembering the breathless scramble up the precipice in the dark when she was a student in the Fourth Ring, she felt grateful to Roger and squeezed his fingers as the curtains rose. Of all the pleasures in her new life, she enjoyed this moment best.

But Roger grew bored with Lincoln Center, City Center, and all the other centers. They stopped going out except for an occasional charity gala. If he must be entertained, Roger preferred to dine out, relaxing over filet mignon with mushroom caps and conversation with old business friends. Actually, and Penny quite understood his desires, he preferred most to stay home.

Roger had not expected to have another child. "There's no return on it," he had often said about his first family. Even before the divorce, his own children had been turned against him. The son hardly spoke to Roger, and the daughter rarely saw him without asking him for a horse or a trip to Colorado or some other cruelly exploitive gift. He had been too busy making his way as a young stockbroker to enjoy the company of his children when they were small. Looking now at their baby pictures, little Bob lying naked on a fur coat with the soft red face of an alcoholic, little Sylvie a froth of ruffles, clutching a toy giraffe, he realized his mistake.

Penny conceived immediately. In her last months of pregnancy the swelling roundness of her abdomen suggested both a Madonna and the tummy of a pre-adolescent child. Inspired, Roger began making more money than he had ever made before with far less effort.

They named the baby Victoria. Visitors to the Barlow House nursery were enchanted by the sight of the delicious infant standing in her stretch terry jumpsuit at nine and a half months, holding tightly to the bars of her crib, her image reflected many times in the mirrors still hung around the walls of her room. Later she would toddle from wall to wall, passionately kissing her own image. "Look at this child's remarkable instep," Roger would say, seizing hold of one chubby leg and pointing the foot at the visitor. "A born dancer."

Rory was a stubborn infant. When displeased she would draw her thick brows together and scowl. In her second year she was impossible. Once Rory threw herself down on the marble floor in front of the main desk of the Jefferson Market Library; passersby were forced to step over her to reach the elevator. Unable to budge her child, Penny began to weep.

One day when Rory was almost three, Penny took a notion to have a haircut. She timidly entered the elegant-looking salon a bit further down on Tenth Street and emerged a strikingly handsome woman. "This is more modern, eh?" the Italian hairdresser said proudly, staring at her sleek thoroughbred head in the mirror. "The long hair, the braids, it's for a stage play, yes?" He kissed his fingers to her in the mirror. "Now you are real life."

Roger objected to the haircut. "You could have told me first."

"But I didn't know you would mind."

"You look completely different. I mind that you want to look like someone else."

But Roger grew used to her new look, enjoyed watching other men admire his elegant wife in passing. He gave her little feasting glances in restaurants. He bought her gemstones for a necklace at an excellent price.

"How would you feel if I had my front tooth capped?"

"Of course, do it. If it bothers you . . ."

Roger hated to admit the feeling, even to himself. When

Penny returned from the dentist with a more dazzling smile, he found he preferred the old imperfect one; it was more dear.

Although the role of a beauty was difficult for her, Penny worked at it with the same diligence she had used for her port de bras. Any spare time away from Rory she spent on facials, manicures, saunas, wardrobes. The mothers of other little girls soon looked at her with mistrust as she turned up outside Humpty Dumpty Playschool in a short red-velvet jacket and jaunty red cap. Women, she thought, have always been jealous of me. It's lucky I have found Roger.

Her best friend was her hairdresser, Gian-Carlo, who had changed her life in such a startling way. He would reminisce about his underpaid but more poetic life in Napoli, and she would comfort him, saying things like, "You can't go home again." As her taste developed, she wore more daring clothes: harem pants, trapezoids, mitred stripes, bare midriffs. With her lithe figure she could bring off anything. At the playground mother and daughter wore matching burnt-sienna velour jumpsuits with asymmetrical zippers and oversized burnt-sienna berets. Among the toddlers in their fraying snowsuits and mothers in bulky down jackets, they looked as exotic as visiting Venusians.

Rory grew up to look pretty much like Roger, thick dark hair, thick dark eyebrows, solid burgherlike figure with broad shoulders and strong thighs. "She'll make a great swimmer," the lifeguard at Southampton said when she was still in diapers, and like a good fairy's wish, the prediction came true. She swims superbly.

Roger and Penny gradually stopped being happy together, so slowly that they hardly noticed when it came about. Roger felt sad when he realized that Penny whom he had always treasured infuriated him. "She's inarticulate is the problem," he told his therapist. To himself he thought, "She's a drag." Sometimes when she hadn't been able to deal with tradespeople, make excuses for an invitation, or when she allowed herself to get stuck with a bore at a party, Roger would berate her, and she would look up at him with such a dumbstruck, helpless expression that he wanted to strike her. "I know I'm a brute," he told Dr. Greenberg. "I just can't control myself."

Penny was inarticulate but not incapable of action. One midnight when she and Roger were having an argument and Roger said, "I picked you up out of the gutter," she picked up a Steuben glass vase etched with a scene from Romeo and Juliet and threw it at Roger's head. Luckily Roger ducked. The vase missed but shattered one of the tall mirrors; it took an hour to clean up the shards. From that moment, Roger never felt the same about Penny, nor she about him. For a long time, whenever Penny thought about her husband, she felt a swarming in her brain, and all she could formulate was, "He has lost his magic."

Roger and Penny still live in Barlow House, Roger on the fourteenth floor in another of his apartments, a one bedroom with terrace. To visit Dad all Rory has to do is step down the brown-carpeted hallway and press the stainless steel button; an elevator whisks her up seven flights.

Although Penny carries herself very regally as she goes about her errands in the Village, she is no longer the most striking woman on line at Balducci's. All winter long she suffers from upper respiratory infections and sinusitis, spending long hours indoors working jigsaw puzzles and doing petit point. Ever since Gian-Carlo returned to Italy she's let her hair grow back and wears it up, as she once did onstage. She is not interested in marrying again. She has completely lost her stretch.

Roger, on the other hand, works out on the Nautilus machines at the Gotham Health and Racquet Club and looks fit and boyish. When he and Penny meet in the elevator as they sometimes do, and walk out the front door together, they seem like a couple of approximately the same age.

Rory is eleven now, a quick, articulate child who loves her Daddy dearly. Every morning at 8 A.M. a brand-new bus from Educational Travel bears her off to a private school on the Upper East Side and returns her to Barlow House at 5:45. Besides swimming three times a week with her coach, she takes a full academic program as well as after-school activities: tennis, ballet, and Chinese cooking. She is also interested in skating, both ice and roller. She is too sensible to want a pony. On weekends Roger and Rory go skiing and when in town see a movie and have an Italian or Chinese meal.

Because Roger loves his daughter immoderately, he is only moderately unhappy. At the office when he thinks of Rory, a smile comes to his lips. Despite the high cost in personal hardship, he says, he feels his involvement in this particular marriage paid off.

Gypsy Ways

That night in October 1962, even the smallest things went wrong from the start. My best friend, Franny, and her husband, Jean-Pierre, were invited for dinner. I spent the whole day preparing an elegant dish from *Mastering the Art of French Cooking*, and after endless stirring, whisking, and reducing, I produced one tiny bowl of *coquilles* that had no taste at all.

Why was I making such a fuss on Franny's behalf, when at her house we always ate tuna fish or Stouffer's frozen chicken tetrazzini? For eight years I had been under Franny's spell, and now that she had married, my enchantment had not weakened. I was twenty-two then and living for the first time in my own apartment. All my old college friends had married and now presided over full sets of Lenox china, Baccarat crystal, and parquet cheeseboards. Whenever I visited them, their new husbands would be mixing drinks in shiny cocktail shakers from Georg Jensen, and the tables would be laid with Belgian linen. Even their garbage cans seemed elegant and glossy. Although I didn't have expensive wedding presents or a husband, I, too, spent lots of time cooking.

The Ferauds, unlike the other couples I knew, were down on their luck. Jean-Pierre was out of a job, and Franny's rich mother had recently cut off her allowance. The Ferauds didn't have any wedding presents because they had never married: Jean-Pierre already had a wife in France. This arrangement shocked those in the Dutchess college class of '59 who came to know their secret.

Although in many ways the Ferauds were a couple ahead of their time (what we then called Bohemian), their domestic life remained perfectly conventional. Franny automatically took Jean-Pierre's name when they signed the lease on their apartment, and she also took his shirts to the Chinese laundry, laughed at all his jokes, and treated him like a treasure beyond price, just as all my other classmates did with *their* husbands. Although her monthly clothing allowance had been bigger than his whole salary, Franny was even more submissive and worshipful than most young wives. Her pet name for Jean-Pierre was Fluffy, and he called her Feather.

Jean-Pierre was an actor, or he had been an actor, or he said he had been an actor. In any case, his thick accent made it hard for him to get work. For a while he sold men's clothing at Saks Fifth Avenue; then he quit to direct a boutique, but the store never opened. Because of his long legs and slim build, he looked wonderful in expensive clothes, though he wasn't in truth handsome.

Jean-Pierre had a careless, mercurial nature, very suited to an actor, I suppose, but out of place in retail trade. When he came home, he would drop his $250 celery-colored jacket on the floor and kick it into a corner, because he felt the United States was destroying his talent. Although he always looked better after sleeping in his clothes than most men do dressed up for a party, he bathed infrequently and often forgot to cut his fingernails. Franny would clip his nails tenderly and shampoo his coarse, black hair. She would tip a kitchen chair backward against the sink, then massage his scalp vigorously, just as a hairdresser would.

Of course, despite her good care, Jean-Pierre was rough and inconsiderate to Franny, but this only increased her devotion. She would often tell me of some mean action of his with a special beatific smile, as though it didn't make any difference to her. "You mean he ripped up your best nightgown?" I would cry in disbelief. A lot of clothes in Franny's wardrobe were ripped, for one reason or another, but she never seemed to mind. She, too, was bone-thin and elegant-looking; she really wore size one.

After I found out about the ripped clothes, I didn't know how to treat Jean-Pierre. But then, I never knew how to treat any of my friends' husbands. I didn't want to seem too interested in them, yet I was highly interested. I was studying husbands, trying to figure out what gave them their special appeal.

If I could locate the common denominator, perhaps I would get married, too.

On that October evening, the Ferauds were almost an hour late, but I was used to their ways and spent the time fruitfully, arranging my furniture carefully, moving my Rya rug around from place to place, putting gay touches of flowers here and there. I remember standing in the doorway, trying to re-imagine the living room as a stranger would see it and deciding that a very charming and tasteful person must live here.

When they arrived, Franny and Jean-Pierre burst into the room with cheerful enthusiasm and made a tremendous fuss about my new arrangements. What good company they were: they were never troubled by self-doubts or embarrassment; they were never dreary or depressed. They loved everything! They would strike up conversations about art with the Good Humor man after praising his popsicles or invite their dentist home for chili in lieu of paying their bills. After dinner, they'd make the dentist totally happy by plying him with eager questions about the best way to floss their teeth.

"We've invited someone for dinner. We knew you wouldn't mind," Franny said, while hanging up her shawl. "We told him what a great cook you are!"

"It's Hubert, an old schoolfriend of mine—a regular guy!" added Jean-Pierre, whose American slang always sounded peculiar. I often wondered if he learned it from a dictionary.

"Also, please don't be angry," said Franny, swiftly falling down on her knees and clasping her hands before her. "We can't stay for dinner. We're invited to a party."

It is hard to get angry at someone down on her knees before you, as Franny very well knew, but before I could expostulate about all the trouble this dinner had caused me, the doorbell rang.

Although Jean-Pierre and Hubert had been schoolboys together in Paris, they hadn't met or corresponded for many years but had run into each other by chance only that morning. Hubert was a solemn-looking bearded man, as quiet in his manner as the Ferauds were exuberant. He was roughly dressed in a plaid shirt and dungarees, as if for farm chores. Fashion has changed so much since then that it's hard to believe that I thought his costume eccentric. Because he was a graduate student at N.Y.U., he should have been wearing a charcoal-gray suit, perhaps with a vest.

"Hubert is homesick and low on dough," said Jean-Pierre, as Hubert glowered in embarrassment. "So I said, why not come to dinner with us tonight? Our friend Sally is a terrific hash-slinger."

"Dinner tonight is very poor," I announced quickly, to lower expectations.

"Let's eat lightly, because there'll be plenty of food at the party. It's actually a dinner party," confessed Franny without a sign of remorse. "We were going to arrive a little late and eat twice."

"What kind of business is this?" I exclaimed. Yet somehow I could never work up enough fury to yell at Franny. Since I knew she was completely unreliable and I loved her anyway, I felt I had no right to complain. Spending time with her was like going to live with the Gypsies.

I loved the way she sneaked library books out singly in her handbag and sneaked them back again twice a year by suitcase. I could never do that. I loved to hear her tell wicked things she had done at debutante parties.

"It's our old classmate, Muffy," she explained, "who's married a Broadway producer. We met her in the park this afternoon. It's a once-in-a-lifetime chance for Jean-Pierre to get a play."

"Actually, we'd better leave right now," said Jean-Pierre, briskly putting his coat back on. "But it was worth coming, really, just to see your new living room. What a miracle! Hubert, old pal, you stay here with Sally. Back in a jiffy!"

"Be nice to each other, children," Franny called as she charged after Jean-Pierre. "Ciao!"

So that was that. I removed one place setting, lit the candles, and sat down to dinner and a bottle of expensive white wine with Hubert Pujot.

Our situation may appear to have an element of romance: available single woman dining by candlelight with Gallic stranger, soon to be her lover or perhaps, later on, her spouse. The truth is, Hubert refused to flirt. Perhaps he was paralyzed by shyness, which I mistook for arrogance or indifference. Perhaps he was congenitally quiet.

Whatever the reason for his silence, our table conversation soon took on the aspect of a police interrogation, Hubert spooning up his *marmite de légumes* as I queried him about his life and expectations. Before each answer, he would sigh wearily.

Hubert was the first man I ever met who wore work shoes socially. To my astonishment, he moved to the living room after dinner and put his high-laced boots up on my beige velveteen sofa. Then, yawning and stretching and confessing that he wasn't used to drinking so much wine, he snuggled his imposing head against my corduroy pillows and fell asleep.

Feeling terrible, I cleared up and washed the dishes, then reconciled my checkbook for the month, while time slowly passed. By 11:30 I had rearranged and straightened everything I owned and was just sitting down to another helping of my orange mousse when Franny reappeared.

"Where's Jean-Pierre?"

"Oh, the party was a disaster! Good thing you decided not to come. Completely boring, terrible food, and Roy wasn't a producer at all, just a rich guy who invested in a few plays. Mummy gave more to the Met than he ever made on Broadway."

"Where's Jean-Pierre?"

"He's waiting down in Lorna and Edward's car. They were

the only decent people there, and they invited us back to their place for a drink. How's Hubert?"

I pointed to the mound on the sofa. "He's not his usual lively self."

Franny raised her eyes to the ceiling. "I'm not sure we have room for him in the car."

"Well, you can't leave him here. Where did you find him anyway?"

"At the post office." Franny walked over and stroked Hubert's cheek. "Rise, my little cabbage leaf," she cooed, and Hubert smiled and rose to his feet obediently. I believe he woke up, too, though his actions for the rest of the evening don't bear out this interpretation.

"Aren't you coming, Sally? Lorna is dying to see you."

"Well, it's late, and I have an appointment tomorrow." I was furious with Franny for accepting everyone's hospitality but mine and ruining my evening in the bargain. While waiting, however, I had successfully rearranged my feelings along with everything else, so I didn't feel angry, just very tired. "Why can't they come here?"

"Lorna has a baby-sitter waiting. We're only going to stay an hour, I promise you, and we'll bring you right home."

"No, I can't."

"Oh, do come along, Sally. You never let yourself have any fun."

"I like fun as much as you do," I said, exasperated. "But I have to catch the ten o'clock bus to New Jersey tomorrow. My grandmother's nursing home is having an art show, and I promised to go weeks ago."

"All the more reason to enjoy yourself now," Franny coaxed, grabbing my hand and pressing it with her long, elegant fingers. "I swear we'll bring you home in an hour."

"You're sure Jean-Pierre will walk me home? He won't be too tired? We have to walk past *your* house to get to *my* house."

"Word of honor as a Girl Scout!"

By chance our various apartments were lined up like milestones on Central Park West. I lived at 96th, Franny lived at 103rd, and Lorna lived at 109th. I don't know what it's like in that part of the city now, but at that time there was a sharply demarcated line of safety; the residents below 96th could stroll about in the evening walking their dogs in front of their large apartment houses, nodding benevolently to their doormen. It was easy to get a taxi, day or night.

Above 96th Street everything changed. The side streets were miserable slums, and menace overhung the sidewalks. Most of the apartment houses on upper Central Park West were still impressive-looking, but they lacked doormen; after sundown tenants scuttled in behind their locked lobby doors. Nowadays I believe crime is more homogenized, and one takes care wherever one goes. In 1962 the Ferauds lived in a well-known No-Man's-Land, and after dark no matter how broke they were, Franny always carried a ten dollar bill to appease muggers.

In the backseat of the Karmann-Ghia, I endured being squashed against Hubert with dignity. I was too busy talking to Lorna, whom I rarely met. She'd been the only black girl in our college class (in those days, of course, we always said "Negro"). Since Lorna was no darker than I was when I came back from a week in Acapulco and since her father was a wealthy property owner, she hardly even counted as a token Negro.

I had always been drawn to Lorna, but she never allowed me to know her well. She was pretty, soft-spoken, always agreeable, but she never mentioned her feelings or hopes, and her mild eyes always seemed anxious. I remember naively wondering why Lorna was so reserved, even though in the only revealing remark she'd ever made, she told me that the kids in high school in Chicago used to tease her and call her Pinky.

In college Lorna had a dazzling succession of boyfriends from Yale, Harvard, and Princeton, all stars in sports or science or handsomer than Harry Belafonte. All appeared as if by magic through a network of black friendships. We were madly envious of Lorna's social life in the Ivy League, though no one would really have wanted to change places with her.

Edward, the man she had finally married, seemed a jovial, likable fellow, though in no way a star. He was a junior attorney in a large law firm—steady, reliable, a man on his way up. As a matter of fact, he became Assistant Commissioner of Human Rights in New York City and is now something important in Washington.

I began to feel uneasy as we parked in front of the Blakes' arsenal-like building, and the very first thing I saw lying on the sidewalk just outside the lobby was a single, well-polished woman's shoe.

"Look, isn't that creepy?" said Franny. "You just know someone got raped or murdered."

"Maybe just drunk," said Jean-Pierre. "You guys worry too much."

"Our neighbor got mugged at the door only last week," said Edward cheerfully. "Somebody stuck a gun in his back just as he put his key in the lock."

"We're only staying here till Stephanie goes to school," said Lorna. "It's a shame, because the apartment is really nice."

The Blakes' apartment was indeed nice—six enormous airy rooms with enough space in the front hall for a large English perambulator. "Occasionally we hear a bloodcurdling scream from the street, but we just pay no attention," said Edward, opening his large, well-stocked bar.

At first I found it pleasant to drink and chat and examine the Blakes' well-designed furnishings. Edward enthusiastically showed us his ships-in-bottles collection, which lined the shelves on one white wall of the living room; they were handsome, white-sailed clipper ships.

"When we got engaged, I told my father that Edward owned twenty-two valuable ships." Lorna laughed. "And he was very impressed. Edward knows how to build them, too. The great moment comes when you pull the string and the whole ship springs up."

I don't remember what we were drinking—something old and expensive from a sparkling crystal decanter. Jean-Pierre in very high humor began swapping outrageous stories with Edward, who turned out to be a very garrulous storyteller himself. Jean-Pierre told stories about niggers, and Edward told stories about frogs. Then Jean-Pierre did an imitation of Edward driving (for the first time I believed that Jean-Pierre might have been an actor, after all), which was so hysterical that even Hubert smiled.

For a while we danced. I danced with Edward, then with Jean-Pierre, finally with Franny, since Hubert wouldn't get up from his chair. By dancing, I mean holding on to each other, the way we did back then.

After the rest of us sat down, Jean-Pierre and Franny continued dancing, this time a mock-tango, breathing each other's breath, nibbling each other's neck, and grinding their lower regions. They never seemed to run out of energy, and the Blakes' living room, like a giant stage, was big enough for all kinds of swoops and flourishes.

"They're so thin, their bones must knock against each other in bed," Lorna remarked, as they sailed around the room, laughing. "They'll crack their pelvises. Tell me," she continued in a sharpened voice, "would you give up a fortune to live with Jean-Pierre? He's so lightweight, he's air."

I stared at Lorna in astonishment. Marriage had changed her, I thought. I had never heard her make a critical comment before.

"Jean-Pierre can be very charming," I answered lamely. It seemed dishonorable to criticize the husbands of one's friends, like an insult to the tribe. And it left oneself open to insult. After all, didn't Lorna realize that her Edward was pompous as well as jovial? All husbands had something wrong with them, I sadly thought.

After a while I began saying wearily at ten-minute intervals,

"When are we going to leave?" but no one paid the slightest attention. I can't claim I was surprised. I decided to appeal directly to Franny when I caught her alone in the kitchen.

"Look, you promised you'd leave in an hour, Girl Scout oath!"

Franny fixed me with her large, expressive eyes. "Oh, Sally, please don't spoil everything! We don't want to offend Edward. He just mentioned getting Jean-Pierre a job in his law office."

"What on earth will Jean-Pierre do in a law office?"

"How can you say that? Jean-Pierre's intelligent. He can do anything anyone else can do. Why don't you ask Hubert to take you home? He's free."

I had forgotten all about Hubert, who was still slumped in his chair in the darkest corner of the living room. Swallowing my pride, I approached. "How would you like to walk me home, Hubert?"

He stared at me with his beady little eyes.

"I'll give you some orange mousse. You had some for dessert, remember? Made with genuine Grand Marnier? Are you alive or not?"

He shook his head, no.

Since I had no alternative, I moved to Jean-Pierre, who was now arm wrestling Edward at the dining room table. They had taken off their jackets and rolled up their shirtsleeves. Edward's shoulders looked twice as broad as Jean-Pierre's, but Jean-Pierre was winning and laughing loudly about it. His hair was plastered in damp little curls on his forehead.

"I'd really like to go home now, Jean-Pierre. I have to get up early tomorrow. Franny promised we wouldn't stay more than an hour."

"Fuck off!"

For the first time in my life I wished I was strong enough to knock down a man. Full of impotent wrath, I went to the living room windows and stared out at the empty street. I saw little traffic, no people. I stood there for a few minutes. Then a lighted taxi flashed by. Great, good, another will come, I said to myself. Although I wasn't crazy about going out among the muggers, I could lurk safely in the vestibule until I saw the light of a taxi and then dash into the street. I slipped quietly into the bedroom to fetch my things. Before I put on my coat, some instinct made me check my handbag. My change purse was missing.

Either I had left my money and keys at home, or someone had stolen them. But who? There wasn't an extensive choice of suspects. Certainly I had left the change purse at home. But I remembered leaving the kitchen light on as usual, then locking the front door carefully; I always put my key inside my change purse. I am a very careful person.

I couldn't believe it. I replaced my coat and went weakly back to the living room.

Lorna was dancing by herself to the mock-calypso blasting from the stereo, waving her slender arms a little crazily, jerking her head.

Yell-ow bird, up in bahn-ahn-a tree,
Yell-ow bird, up in bahn-ahn-a tree.

"Lorna, you're a kind person. Listen—" But she paid no attention. As she waved her arms, she gave me a malicious look.

"What? Still here?" Jean-Pierre said, strolling past with Edward. "Not out on the sidewalk yet?"

"No, I'm still here."

"Not dismembered yet?"

Edward thought this very funny. "I disremember the dismembering."

"Disbarred is more like it, old fellow!"

I refuse to beg them, I thought to myself. I will wait here until they sober up, however long it takes, but I won't beg.

"You're not drinking. Dear me."

Edward clinked his crystal decanter and the liquid poured over my legs. I said nothing. I have never done anything to you, Edward, I thought silently. You always seemed like a nice chap. No Harry Belafonte, but a decent sort.

"Make yourself comfortable, Sally. You're going to be here a very long time." I let Jean-Pierre lead me to the sofa, then roll me backward against the cushions. I felt on the verge of crying out, but I made silence a matter of life and death and clenched my teeth. He's just like some anonymous caller, I told myself. Telling him to stop will only make him persevere, simply to hear your little, piping, begging, screaming voice.

Jean-Pierre put a cushion on my stomach. "This will make you feel better." He piled another on my breasts. He was covering me with cushions.

"You're burying poor Sally. Why are you burying poor Sally?" said Lorna's shrill, sympathetic voice as she piled a pillow on my head, and another on my arms, and another.

I was completely buried. The nubbly pillows across my face scratched me, but I felt it important to keep my eyes open. They are going to kill me, I thought in bemused astonishment. They are going to kill me for no reason.

One thing I did not hear was my best friend Franny's voice. I heard no one crying, "Stop, rescue my friend!" I heard some giggling and unidentifiable squeals, then felt something cobwebby and light, like a shawl, falling on my hair.

Next I felt a heavy weight. Somebody was sitting on me, a massive weight pressing down. Jean-Pierre was sitting on me, or perhaps it was Edward. How would I ever find out? Then the weight grew heavier—insupportably heavier: Franny sitting on Jean-Pierre's lap? I endured the pressure, pretending it was some large, overweight lover, whom I doted on. I tried not to think about earth-covered coffins.

Some tears rolled out of my eyes, and I was glad my face was covered. The other humiliations of the evening—they had not really touched me. I never knew what being humiliated was like until that moment.

Then came such an earsplitting stamping and shouting—

Edward's loud karate cries, wild French curses, and a splinter-
ing as if of wood or perhaps telephone books being ripped
apart. Heels stamping, caterwauling, finally an end-of-the-
world, all-glass crashing. I knew without seeing that Edward's
prized, perfect ships-in-bottles had each and every one of
them been smashed to the floor. Edward had done it, or Jean-
Pierre. I was glad I would never know.

Next I heard a baby howling and bulletlike scolding and re-
criminating. Lorna scolding Franny for forcing Edward to
drink. Franny defending Jean-Pierre in shrieks. A cannonlike
knocking on the door—bang bang bang. Tough but casual
male voices: "Complaints from the neighbors—have to keep it
down." The cops!

I crept out from under my pillows ready to be rescued, but
there was no longer anything to be rescued from. The police
were leaving. Edward and Lorna were down on their knees in
a garbage heap, salvaging. Edward had the sense to look
sheepish; Lorna just looked sick and yellow-eyed.

Not Jean-Pierre. He sat in an armchair, drained but satisfied,
at rest in his dressing room after a long, exhausting performance. Franny sat lightly perched on the arm, her face snuggled against his shoulders. She didn't look at me. Hubert also
had his eyes closed.

Without exchanging a word, we four put on our coats and
walked out to the sidewalk. The lone shoe was still lying there,
but it had lost its horror in the pale light of an up-coming sun.
We trailed down Central Park West as if on our way to an exe-
cution: Jean-Pierre and Franny, three paces ahead, holding
hands, then me, then Hubert, three paces behind. As we
walked, Jean-Pierre kept chattering. I wish I could remember
what he said, something quite ordinary.

No one mugged us.

"You see?" said Jean-Pierre.

When the Ferauds reached their door, Jean-Pierre stopped
and turned toward me inquiringly. I took great pleasure in

walking past him without breaking my stride. Hubert continued following me down Central Park West, although they shouted after him, "Hubert, come up for a few minutes!" The last I saw of Hubert as I ducked into my apartment building, he was walking south.

After all this time I am still puzzled about Hubert. Was he on dope? Was he an early example of the anomie of the sixties? Or was he simply depressed when he realized that he was spending the evening with a hated childhood bully? Perhaps Jean-Pierre had washed his face with snow once too often or poured itching powder down his shirt. Homesickness can be carried too far.

The doorman let me in. My change purse, as I suspected, was not to be found anywhere at home. On Monday Franny sent me an expensive florist's box of yellow roses with a neat white card: "Sally, forgive me! I don't know what I do!"

Although I never spoke another word to Jean-Pierre, Franny and I continued in the guise of friends for several months, meeting for picnics and walks in the park. Then in 1963, Franny and Jean-Pierre separated; Franny left New York to live in various places around the globe—Majorca, Marrakesh, Nepal. Meanwhile I had found a husband and had a baby. Soon I had another baby. By then I could hardly believe that I was the same person who had once been uncomplainingly smothered with pillows.

One day when a long letter from Franny arrived from Taxco describing in eloquent detail the sky and mountains but without mentioning whom she was traveling with or when she was coming home, I suddenly grew very angry. Without thinking much about it, I never answered any of her letters or saw her again.

Who Could Love
a Fat Man?

When we first met, I could not bear to look at Archie. I found his cheeks too thick, his head too round, his figure unappealing. Although his voice was pleasant enough, he had a foolish laugh. To disoblige him, I entered into a lighthearted conversation about his name, wishing perhaps to pinpoint his weaknesses and use him for a funny story on another day. Sportingly, I let him see my malice in sharp explosive laughter between my smiles. Sportingly, he ignored my malice and began to talk about the origins of *my* name. The story he invented (as I later found when I checked at the public library) was clever; I found him quick and articulate. We stood for a long time talking in the street, while the friend who introduced us leaned negligently against a wall.

We agreed to go to dinner together at a later date, and I remember glancing backward at his plump figure trundling down the street. An obscure restaurant, dark in corners, I thought, not wishing to link myself too closely with such a shape. I neglected to notice how readily I had accepted Archie's invitation. His last name was Boggan, his profession, a writer of fiction.

On the day of our engagement, I boldly decided to break it and, unaware of his habits, called him at noon, waking him from what he later described as his "best sleep." His voice, ruffled like an owl's, sounded vague and harassed.

"It is I," I said grandly.

"Who are you?" he replied, prowling about a bit for the proper register. "Do I know you?"

Suspecting some artifice (how many women could Archie possibly know?), I laughed into the receiver and waited for the shock of recognition. I was used to playing foul then, because of nervous problems which could not interest you.

"What number do you want?" he muttered.

"It's Myra. About tonight, I don't think I can come."

"Oh, yes, of course. If you like," he deferred. It was my affair, the voice implied.

"How about tomorrow?" I astonished myself by suggesting. Later I was always astonished at my impulsive clutch on him as he slipped away, assenting mildly to my rejection.

"If you want to," he replied.

"I would like to. Yes."

Archie led a peculiar life for a bachelor of thirty. He rose every afternoon at about two, and after breakfasting on three slices of French toast with real maple syrup, he donned his father's old camel's hair coat for a stroll in Central Park. Of course he looked foolish, and perhaps I should have mentioned this earlier. His fluffy blond hair sprayed up in front and his shabby blond belt sagged down in back as he walked leisurely around the reservoir, pausing for deep healthy breaths. He looked like a straggler, a remnant from another era, which I suppose he was. He walked surrounded by young mothers with baby carriages into which he peered, and old ladies on benches at whom he smiled, and a few young thugs in leather jackets whom he did not acknowledge. He cut a remarkable, aimless figure. He looked like a recent failure, for his father's coat had once been very expensive, and no one could believe that his portly body and plumpish cheeks were not well cared for. "A bachelor, somebody's mother's boy—selfish and eccentric," some sharp-skinned old lady on a bench might think. But Archie was an orphan and had not been pampered even when his parents lived, and they had died when he was sixteen.

He lived alone in a dark, labyrinthine rent-controlled apartment inherited from his long-dead parents and still choked with their paintings and heavy furniture and his mother's twenty-year-old pipe-organ cactus. After dawdling through the park and then perhaps the Metropolitan Museum, he would stop at his neighborhood Key Food and gather a bouquet of stuffed paper bags, which he would bring back to his dark, empty, crowded rooms. After showering and shaving, he would cook himself a sumptuous lunch of meat, gravy, and instant whipped potatoes. I found his living room littered with bowls of chocolate, marzipan, and nonpareils, with half-empty boxes of raisins and plump strings of figs. He was also fond of Mister Salty Veri-Thin Pretzels.

At our second meeting, I again found Archie appealing and repellent at the same time. Still, I felt less brittle, and it seemed to be because of Archie. At least I did not think of repeating our conversation for a third person's delight. Although I shifted nervously in my chair, smoked a pack of Camel Lights, and drummed the table with my fingertips, he appeared not to notice. He bought me dinner and cocktails and seemed anxious that I enjoy myself.

Afterward we took a ferry to Staten Island, past the deep well-like lights around the Statue of Liberty. The boat ride was Archie's idea, and because the starry river became an ideal setting for a new, attractive Archie, I again suspected a trick. You see, it was cold. The river wind chilled me; beside me stood Archie, his camel-coated body solid with warmth and a fervent afterdinner humor. How he enjoyed the view, his large Saxon head swinging round with delight, peering back to the lights and then back to me, comfortable inside and out, all unified with pleasure.

He warmed my hands in his sagging pockets and talked for a long time in a soft introspective New York voice, mentioning in an unstressed way, welded as it were, into the framework of the conversation, the possibility of his love. I was a damned clever woman, he said, for someone so well put together. Since there were no joints or seams in his monologue, after he went on to something else, I lingered on his early words, concentrating all my attention on them. I wanted him to return to the subject of love, but he would or could not. When the boat docked, I wanted what was suddenly coming to me. We necked all the way uptown in a taxi. You think I was won too easily? I was ripe, that's true.

The next morning I tended to dwell on the romantic moments of the ferry ride, but when I noticed my pleasure at some stars, some water, and a few careless words, I laughed at myself and went back to work. (You think I am some college girl, starsick and silly? I am, I'm proud to tell you, the curator of a small museum in Brooklyn, head of the whole thing at twenty-eight.) I have been humiliated by too many miserable love affairs to suffer once again for Archie. I recalled his rumpled clothing and the mottled red on his forehead where the wind had caught his face. After all, who could love a fat man?

My crisis came a few days later when, in a vulnerable moment, I began to daydream about Archie. Perhaps he was different from the other rats. "He is not handsome or transcendent in any way," I thought, "but kind, trustworthy, plain. He appreciates me."

Unfortunately, Archie did not call again. From past experience I expected a power play, but I could not believe that Archie would resort to such a maneuver. I laid blame for his disappearance on his shyness, his fragile dignity. He was not the sort to pursue a woman.

Archie was not shy. What protective mechanism made me think of shyness? On the following evening at six o'clock he appeared without invitation at my door, flushed and smiling, pleased about some small success (the "sale" of a story to some obscure, nonpaying literary quarterly). "Celebrations, wine!" he cried happily, resting expectantly against the door frame. In his arms he held a brown paper bag, a silvered bottle protruding from the opening. Two high spots of color burned his cheeks.

"Why didn't you telephone first?" I snapped, snubbing the amiable figure at my door. After all, I had expected a hesitant telephone call, the symbol of courtship, not the brashness of direct attack. "How did you know I was home?" I glared at him for undervaluing me, clutching my shabby bathrobe around me. I saw the rat in every curve of Archie's face.

"It's Tuesday," he replied irrelevantly, shoving over the threshold. "Are you free?"

"All right, I'll get dressed," I muttered in an aggrieved tone, surrendering the point but meaning to hold the advantage.

I lost it immediately, for Archie laughed as I closed the door and advanced toward me, clasping me in the impetuous folds of his overcoat. "I had a dream about screwing you," he murmured in my earlobe, and I yielded from sheer surprise. I remember settling into his fierce embrace with a feeling less of happiness than of willful daring, as though I were plunging gaily off a cliff.

Perhaps Archie's aggressiveness seems out of character. Could Archie have stalked me with greater success if he had been a cool pleasure-seeker, a Don Juan of Central Park? I surrendered to Archie without any declaration, on the strength of hope alone. Had I seen him more than twice in my life? Dress Archie in a clean camel coat with sharp, flat pockets; suppress his fluffy hair with an expensive cut by a topflight stylist; consolidate the vagrant humor in his face, and you have the image of a bland-jawed, smooth-cheeked seducer.

After we became lovers, I began to punctuate Archie's flowing days with unannounced visits, the prerogative of my passion. I requested a key to his apartment, a favor he did not think to ask of me. It pleased me to sit in Archie's apartment with Archie out and the parents dead. I sat in a great brown velvet armchair near the smudged and opaque windows, watching the dust motes fly up from under my restless feet. I heard the bottle flies buzz in the kitchen and thought how clean the dark rooms would be and how inaccessible to me if Archie's mother were still cooking dinners at the end of the long dark hall. It was the photos that set me off on this track, not morbidity, for I wasn't really jealous of the little woman in the dusty gilt frame. Mrs. Boggan had borne her only Archie when she was forty. "Such children are bound to be geniuses or idiots," Archie had informed me serenely, sweeping back his hair to show the faint forceps scars on his forehead. As it was, I never stepped into the kitchen to usurp anybody's place. I let Archie do all the cooking, and it was spring before I dared water her cactus.

Still, we became rather domestic. I spent almost every evening with Archie in his large quiet living room, sitting companionably by his side. At first we talked endlessly. Archie wanted to learn all about me, reassuring proof of his attachment. Though I am naturally a reserved person, I poured out my story several times over; my last lover had been a Don Juan, an alcoholic *and* a married man. I cried on Archie's shoulder. He, in turn, told me of his loneliness, his art, yet the unimportance of literature beside experience and love.

Later on, Archie fell into the habit of reading while I visited. We sat in separate chairs, where I could watch his silent, rapid breathing in the dusty blue mirrors which his mother, because she was vain or fashionable, had hung all about the room. Yet even when Archie seemed most engrossed in his paperback, he would take his pencil and write a few words on the end papers, sighing as with enormous effort. Like any neglected woman, I would put questions to him, turn and fiddle with the stereo, open and close windows, anything to make him remember me.

Sometimes he would leave me to fetch a glass of milk and amble his way down the narrow corridor to the kitchen. I would hear his heavy footsteps and the amazed, ineffectual sound of the refrigerator door. When I followed him, some minutes later, I would find him lost in contemplation, his hand resting on the glass-topped kitchen table, the milk container beside it. He would smile, drink quickly, and follow me back to the books and mirrors.

Now we might have continued in this equivocal fashion for months or even years, since our sexual relations were more than satisfactory, and we never quarreled, except for one oc-

currence for which I was entirely unprepared. Archie became
a success before my eyes.

It would be inaccurate to say that I didn't believe in Archie's
writing. Of course I believed in it. I merely did not imagine
that anyone else would like it, too. The returned manuscripts
which appeared occasionally in Archie's mailbox had always
seemed to me sufficient proof of his authorship. And just as I
always looked upon Archie's writing as an indoor occupation,
something pleasant he did to pass the time, I always accepted
Archie himself as a drifting figure without visible means of
support (he had a small, invisible trust fund), as though he had
been born without a paycheck as he had been born without a
cleft chin or without dimples. Imagine my surprise when Archie received a letter from an eminent publisher announcing
that the novel Archie had submitted had won an important
literary prize. He was awarded $10,000 and loud, parental-
sounding praise.

Archie telephoned me as soon as he heard the news, but his
voice was so distorted by joy that at first I hung up in anger; I
thought it was some drunkard who had dialed the wrong number. As soon as I understood that it was Archie, I was pleased
but also disquieted, for I still could not recognize his voice.
With a booming and confident laugh, he spoke of selling his
novel to the movies. That Archie owned such a laugh and had
never used it before seemed to me a sign of deception; it
seemed that Archie had always secretly planned to succeed.

I rushed to see Archie immediately after his telephone call,
full of dread and anticipation. My worst fears were confirmed.
I found that most of the heavy furniture in the living room had
been pushed into the middle of the room and piled upside
down, curved feet pathetically clawing the air. Archie himself
stood in his undershirt at the top of a ladder, energetically pol-
ishing a mirror.

"What are you doing up there?" I cried out idiotically,
shaken by the half-cleaned, disordered room.

"Housecleaning." Archie grinned and waved his dustcloth.

"*What* are you doing?" I cried again. "Come down and talk to me. You never cleaned before."

"I'm giving a party tomorrow," Archie continued. "In behalf of my novel. You can meet all my friends."

"A party." I sank down on the velvet hassock in disbelief. I would have been less surprised if Archie had opened a secret closet and shown me his mad wife. "You never said you liked parties."

I trembled for the end of our quiet life together, and Archie climbed down from his stepladder to comfort me.

"Is that all you're going to do? Give a party?" I muttered.

"Let's go out into the park," he said gently, "and sit on the grass. Did you think I was going to move to Park Avenue and find another girl?"

Luckily the party did not turn out as well as I had feared. I had imagined a flock of sudden friends, worldly people crowding through the door. I expected pretty women. Fortunately, his few friends were shy, bespectacled young doctors and architects with dowdy wives, a respectable showing for a lonely man. They stood in little affiliated clusters and spoke of Archie affectionately. But though his friends got drunk with remarkable speed, they never quite relaxed with him. The only aggressive woman present was Archie's high school English teacher, who wept without embarrassment on Archie's neck.

"Are you Archie's girl?" said one old friend. I nodded to him through the smoke.

"You're lucky," he said patronizingly. "In college we knew he was a genius."

"Yes," I replied, understanding this fact for the first time. "That's true."

At once I felt enormous relief. My discontents did not seem so unreasonable then; everyone knows how difficult it is to get on with a genius.

I fixed my eye on Archie's plump back as he padded among

the noisy guests. "I always knew that Archie was unlike others," I said to the young man.

I stared at Archie as he absently stooped to grab a potato chip. As I watched, the very skin on his face seemed to shift, and a new face grew under it. The strong bones appeared from under the fattish cheek. The line from ear to chin swam to the surface for the first time; I swear it was never there before.

Yet the most remarkable transformation took place only after the party ended. I stood half-hidden behind Archie's shoulder as he said good-bye to the last guest. And as Archie shut the door and turned toward me, I was the only one left over, the only guest with clear permission to stay. I laughed incoherently, as Archie had laughed the day before on the telephone. For that one moment, I was completely happy.

"Don't tell me you're drunk," said Archie with some surprise. "I can't believe it." I leaned forward and rested my forehead against his chest. "I must get you drunk every night," he continued mildly, allowing me to wind my arms around him.

"Unlike others," I whispered.

Archie laughed. "Why are you acting so strangely?" he said.

"Am I?" Hurt by his laughter, I stood up straight again. I put on the light and studied his face. "How do I act?"

"You keep staring at me," he replied steadily, staring at me.

"That's because you're so handsome," I answered, relaxing against him again.

"Don't joke," Archie said. "You stare at me as if you can't quite place me."

"OK, I'll leave. I won't stick around and make you uncomfortable."

Archie made the proper reply. "Don't worry about it," he said. He pulled at the light cord again, and we embraced passionately.

The following evening, Archie and I had our first quarrel. I had decided upon reflection that Archie could best define our relationship by marrying me. Archie had never brought the subject up, I felt sure, because he knew how nervous I was about commitment. He understood how humiliated I would feel if things did not work out. I was shocked, then, when Archie flatly turned me down.

"Please, Myra. Let's not do anything new right now. My novel is at a crucial and delicate point."

"You think more of the novel than you do of me!" This, I confess, was my more than trite reply.

"Well, I can't help it," Archie said in his new bulldozer tone. "I can only do one thing at a time. I've always been like that, and it's too late to change."

"What if I moved in here without our getting married?" I suggested, purely to test his reaction.

No matter how late I stay with Archie, I always go home to change my clothes before work and to brew myself a cup of real coffee. I like to feel independent, as though I have an identity invulnerable to someone else's whim. To be frank, I thought I was making a handsome offer, even though I didn't mean it.

"Well," he said in a maddening conciliatory way. "I would prefer you to stay where you are. I like living alone. Still, if you moved into my parents' room, we could share the rent."

This remark enraged me. "You pay one-third the rent I do, brute, for six times the space. You just won $10,000, and you haven't even thought to buy me a present—a pair of earrings or a cashmere sweater."

I do tend to fall into character assassination when I'm hurt, but then, who doesn't? Nor had Archie ever bought me anything, unless you count the candy bars he sometimes produced from his pockets.

I can hardly bear to record Archie's next remark. "Forget about the earrings," he said. "What if we spent the money on a good analyst for you?"

"You want me to move into your parents' room. You want me to sleep in *their* bed that hasn't even been dusted for fourteen years, and you think that I need a shrink? You're the weirdo, Archie, not me."

Archie made no move to stop me as I fumbled through my purse for his key. Although I intended nothing more than a bluff, the sight of his bland face enraged me further. Without thinking, I threw the key in his face. It rang against a mirror instead.

"You vegetable," I cried. "Can't you even get angry?" Then I raced out of the room.

This scene took place a few days ago, and Archie's mute figure still remains before me. Oddly enough, my feelings have changed in the interval. Archie is an artist, after all, and much can be forgiven him. The room will have to be redecorated, of course; that I insist upon. As for the rent, we'll see about that when the time comes.

I see myself moving toward Archie with all the solemnity and pomp of a coronation. I'll carry no circumspect suitcase but a large plastic bag filled with all my clothes—transparent—open to the neighbors' naked eyes! The enormity of it fills me with awe. The creaky elevator will whirl me to his floor, and when I ring ceremonially, there he will be!

But first I will give Archie a few more days to think over our quarrel, to realize that I may not return. In his loneliness he'll want me; I know it. He may even telephone me first—exhilarating thought. After all, if he didn't love me, he should never have taken up with me in the first place. The responsibility lies with him, isn't that true?

Quintessence of Zoe

Zoe and my husband don't get along. Inadvertently I've told her too much that is evil about my husband, especially just after one of our quarrels. Our battlefield is not the heated steam table of many households but more like the icy wastes of Antarctica; often we don't exchange a word for days, and what is more natural than for me to confide my grievances to my best friend, Zoe?

Unfortunately Zoe arrives unexpectedly one Sunday when the children are visiting friends. Michael and I are at peace, enjoying a few hours of perfect harmony.

"I thought of an idea for a book for you to write," Zoe says as she steps across the threshold, making straight for Michael. She is aggressive and likes to grapple with those who shrink from her. "Nobody has touched the rape of Manchuria."

"Oh, thank you." Michael steps back with mock humility. "Very thoughtful, but don't you think you ought to write your book yourself? I'm just a part-time copy editor. Writing a book is woman's work."

"Why are you teasing me?" Zoe bridles, an impressive action, with short red hair whirling in every direction. "I have always been nice to you. If you put your energy into your work, you'd be more successful than you are now."

"Anyone would be more successful than I am now."

"Oh, he's quick! A quick comeback. How can I top that? You may be ornery, but you're not dumb."

"A draw! I declare this a draw!" I cry, pulling Zoe away from the door and into the living room. I'm sure she has come to talk about her husband, Rolfe, and why she can't divorce him until she finds a high-paying job.

"It's worse than ever." She sits down and begins without preliminaries.

I try to be a supportive listener, but I'm conscious of Michael in our bedroom stewing about his lack of success. Who is going to suffer from that little exchange at the door? Who is going to be available for rapier practice? Over whose dead body will the conflict be resolved?

"Rolfe is an addiction," Zoe says, "and I just have to kick the habit."

"That's a good way to look at it. How'd you think of it?"

"My hairdresser."

Zoe's anguished situation has been keeping her busy for more than two years, and just about everyone she knows except Rolfe has been trying to help her get away from him. Rolfe is so surly and hard to get along with that he makes Michael look wonderful. At least Michael has moments of good humor. When he isn't sulking, he is handy with plumbing and carpentry and fixes things around the house. He has bursts of strong sexual feeling.

According to Zoe, Rolfe is morose, inept, and impotent. Rolfe has his own side of the story to tell, of course, but luckily, we don't get to hear it. He never comes to our parties (oh yes, he's also struggling with a drinking problem), and whenever I visit Zoe he retreats to the garden almost before I am through the door. What's a happy person like Zoe doing with a dark shadow like Rolfe? I always think. I notice his drooping eyelids, his lean depressed jaw, as though he hasn't had a happy moment since World War II. (Rolfe was born in Germany well after the Nazi era and came to this country when he was eight, but it occurs to me that his family could have been murdering my family before we were born.)

"I can't stand it anymore," Zoe says, throwing herself against our sofa pillows with a thump. "Now that Robby is in first grade, I have to make the break. Zoe the Clown has to go."

Here Zoe is talking about her work as a thrower of children's birthday parties. She may be aggressively cheerful and good with kids, and the idea of her own business may have boosted her through several years of failing marriage, but she has outgrown this not very profitable activity and is ready for more challenging things. How is Zoe the Clown going to look on her résumé when she applies for executive status?

"You're lucky, Judy," she says. "You've got a high-paying job."

I think, not for the first time, that Zoe is jealous of her supposed best friend. Has she ever stopped to think that the only reason I'm a hotshot lawyer now is that I kept right on working while I had babies instead of staying home and enjoying them? If she'd ever had to express her milk into the toilet between clients or to stay up all night with a teething infant and then be in court in the morning, she might have a more realistic idea about my "luck."

Truthfully, I could do without my high-paying job, which makes Michael even more jealous than Zoe. A while ago I made a serious mistake. After Michael's first book proposal had been turned down half a dozen times, I advised him to go ahead and quit his job and write it anyway and not worry about the money. Some publisher would be sure to want it. The book has been finished for a year now and shuttling endlessly through the post office. Michael is mad at me and not so ecstatic about my "high-paying job."

"The thing is," Zoe continues, "I've got to make my move now. At our age it's only a short time before we look old—and who's going to hire a middle-aged crone? You can't believe all the time I'm spending keeping in shape to look good. And what's the profit when I feel so awful?"

It's true. Zoe looks good. She's running a lot and taking an aerobic dance class three times a week. Since she's started renewing her hair color she looks better than she did when I first met her in the playground seven years ago.

"In a few years we're going to have dental problems, our children will be disobeying us, our parents will be ailing and crotchety."

"Stop it, Zoe. Stop being so clever and farsighted."

Zoe's comments depress me more than usual. Despite the apparent liveliness of our conversation, we, Michael, Zoe, and I, are no longer young. Each of us has been married before, spent years of our former lives pursuing other domestic unhappiness.

Zoe looks good, but she is now a two-time loser.

At this point Michael wanders back into the living room, ostensibly to get a pencil. It always makes him nervous when Zoe's around, as though she's an agent who's going to seduce me to the other side. "Pay no attention," he says airily, meaning just the opposite.

"I'm just leaving," Zoe replies in a similar spirit.

As soon as Michael goes, Zoe tells me what's really troubling her. "Rolfe is unbelievable." Her face is crumpling. The insouciant air she's maintained through our conversation is gone. "He's sleeping on an air mattress on the sun porch. He says I click my throat when I'm sleeping, that he has to be alone. But he's the one who talks in his sleep."

She clears her throat, drops her voice. "He's violent. He makes threats in his sleep. Last week he thrashed around in our bed and screamed, 'I have a contract out on you!' Then he reached over and grabbed my hand with a grip of iron. I couldn't budge him. I finally had to sock him to wake him up."

I sigh. "That's terrible." Things are much worse for them, have always been much worse.

"Not that I care if he sleeps with me. He's so rotten I'm glad he's away. But it's demeaning, this pallet in the middle of the sun porch. Like he's an old derelict already, which is what he's going to be if he keeps it up.

"I told the children his back was bothering him. They'd believe anything. But if anyone comes to the house, it's apparent what's up. He's humiliating me. He's still listening to my telephone messages. An opthalmologist, for god's sake, sleeping on the floor every night. I've got to get away from him. But he's smart when it suits him, you know, cunning. Can you imagine what kind of settlement I'll get? I've been burned once."

"Is he really violent? I mean, will he harm you?"

"Not unless provoked. I absolutely won't provoke him."

After Zoe leaves, Michael approaches me angrily. His angry stance is icy and disapproving. If I didn't know him so well, I'd think I've done something wrong. "She has a lot of nerve to call me ornery," he says. "That dizzy dame. What have you been telling her?"

"Why be defensive? The whole world knows how sweet-tempered you are."

"Your sarcasm is unnecessary. Why do you let that woman in when we're supposed to be relaxing."

"She's my friend. I can't see her only when convenient. She has big problems now with Rolfe. I wouldn't be surprised if he's heading for a breakdown. He's always been odd."

"If they can't get along, there's no reason for you to get involved. That's the trouble with you women, can't keep your noses out."

I turn away from Michael and go busy myself in the kitchen. Whether Zoe meant to or not, and I'm sure she didn't, she's ruined our tranquillity.

The next morning at 8 A.M. I get a frantic call from Zoe.

"This morning he threatened to stab me."

"Oh, Zoe, why?"

"I told him he was rotten. That I'm going to leave him."

"Oh, Zoe."

"He told me, go ahead, then pulled this bread knife from the table. What a cliché! I ran into the bedroom and I would have called the police, but he raced to the car and drove away. This man is a medical doctor!"

"Do you have the number of that lawyer I gave you? You have to go now, Zoe. You can't wait any longer."

"I've got twenty numbers."

During this conversation, Michael is glaring at me from the hallway. I'm supposed to be braiding Rachel's hair so he can take her to school. I make desperate braiding motions with my hands, which he ignores.

"Go to your mother's right away until you know what's happening."

"What'll I tell her?"

"The truth. If she doesn't know he's a nut by now . . ."

To further unstring the morning, Rolfe calls me at my office. I don't even recognize his name at first, it's such a shock to hear from him. He sounds miserable, perhaps hung over, but he doesn't sound violent.

"I wanted to tell you, Judy, I'm fucking finished with Zoe. If I'm in an accident today, it's no accident. I want to make sure somebody knows that."

"Hold it, Rolfe." This is grand-scale nuttiness, all right. "Why are you telling me this? You want me to tell Zoe so she'll be nicer to you? A relayed threat?"

"No threat, Judy. Privileged information. I happen to like you. If I leave a note, the insurance people will get it."

"I'm not your lawyer, Rolfe. I'm not even your friend, really, but I do know someone you can talk to, a very distinguished Freudian analyst who once helped me a lot."

"Forget the Freudian crap. I'm finished. I've had it. I've had it with Zoe and everyone else. Only I want the boys to have the insurance."

It sounds to me as if Rolfe is serious. I don't know him well enough to know how to dissuade him. He's never been entirely real to me—just a bunch of Zoe's anecdotes.

"Listen, Rolfe, can you meet me for lunch? I'd like to know more about your plans."

"Don't think you can talk me out of it. All you'll do is lose Zoe and the children a lot of money. Anyway, I'm not hungry. I've had my last meal."

I'm trying to think so fast my thoughts are skidding through my head. "How about if you call me back in twenty minutes? I can help you, you know. It's not so easy to stage a suicide to look like an accident."

"Wrong. I've worked it out."

"Are you at home or at the office?"

"Neither." And he hangs up on me.

I call Michael immediately, the one thing I'm not supposed to do in the morning. He would like to write uninterrupted with the telephone shut off, but I won't allow it because the children are in school at the mercy of flying pucks and basketballs, and I'm often unavailable in court. Sometimes Michael doesn't answer the phone anyway.

"What do I care if that sadist kills himself?" Michael replies. "He'll be doing himself a favor. Why did he have to drag you in anyway?"

"I agree. But now I'm in. I'll feel bad if I don't try."

"Look, tell Zoe. It's her problem. What's the point of protecting her? The whole insurance thing is a red herring anyway. It's also conspiracy to defraud."

Here Michael is completely right. That's why I called him.

Luckily Zoe has mentioned that she's running a birthday party at the Prince Edward Hotel from twelve to two. We even spoke of having lunch at their coffee shop, since it's only two blocks from my office, but we decided that the times were wrong.

It's 11:45. I dash over as fast as I can, but I'm not quick enough to catch Zoe. Several parties are scheduled in the hotel, and I don't even know the name of the hosts. I stand uncertainly near the elevators until I see a little boy in a blazer appear with his daddy. He's carrying an elaborately wrapped package—undoubtedly one of Zoe's clientele. I attach myself to the other side of Daddy and follow along. (Daddy looks much happier than Michael would on similar escort duty. He's enjoying himself, chatting with his son, not planning to rush off to the cocktail lounge like Rolfe or scowl at the hosts like

Michael, but then this daddy is a much younger man. His round cheeks gleam; he's born of a different Zeitgeist. He probably goes to weekly parenting classes and once indefatigably helped his wife with her Lamaze breathing in childbed.)

Wearing a brilliant smile, I enter the party room unchallenged and spot Zoe blowing up balloons in a corner of the dining room. She is wearing a pair of Rolfe's trousers held up with crimson suspenders and a giant blue polka-dot bow tie. On her nose is a huge crimson bulb, on her head a green felt hat with a perpendicular flower. She's busy fashioning a little giraffe out of puffy bits of rubber. Eight or nine four-year-olds are squealing around her, and she doesn't appear to be faking her enthusiasm as she asks the children, "And what is this—a duck? Is it a crocodile?" To my astonishment, Zoe looks happy.

Discreetly I try to catch Zoe's eye. Though I move right up and jostle her shoulder, she never glances up. I wait till the balloons are over and the little ones are being shooed over to the dining tables. Zoe is moving toward a puppet theater on the opposite wall.

"Psst. Zoe?"

The clown gives me an amazed annoyed glance.

"I thought you should know that Rolfe just called me and said he was planning an accident this afternoon."

"Here." She ducks behind the puppet screen with me, beyond the public. Despite my frantic breathlessness, I recognize from the stage props that it's a Punch and Judy show.

"What did the bastard say?"

"That he was planning to kill himself this afternoon. But he wasn't going to leave a note."

"A bluff." Zoe is furious. I have always been impressed with the operatic way Zoe acts out her anger—flaring nostrils, flashing eyebeams. "He doesn't have the nerve. He's not the type."

"I wouldn't be too sure, Zoe. He sounded serious."

She wavers. Her intense green eyes widened by circles of white paint glare at me.

"He wouldn't do this to me! Hasn't he ruined my life enough already?"

"Michael and I thought you should know—though what you can do about it now . . . You can try calling the house . . ." All my urgency suddenly seems absurd. "He said he wanted you to have the insurance."

Zoe shakes her head emphatically, and the red paper flower on her hat bobs up and down. "Go home, Judy. It's an idle threat. Who kills himself over a divorce?"

"It's possible."

Zoe overrules me with a haughty toss of her paper flower. "I know my own husband. It's too sensational for him. Besides, he's a coward."

I don't go home. Feeling silly, I go back to the office to prepare a complicated case. A little more than an hour later, Rolfe is killed. He has been to see another eye doctor for an acute complaint. While his vision is still slightly blurry from the examination, he misjudges the edge of the subway platform at Fifth Avenue and falls directly in the path of an oncoming IND train. Rolfe's accident disrupts service for two hours and is featured in the *New York Post* as a lesson to passengers. Only three people in the world know the details of his superb performance.

Michael is kind to me that night. He stays up late with me, listening to my guilty mutterings, telling me soothing and comforting lies. "You handled it beautifully," he says, "but what can you do with a nut?"

On the telephone Zoe is operatically calm. She's taken so many tranquilizers her voice sounds ironed out, without inflection. "I misjudged him," she says eight or nine times, and "What else could I have done?" She doesn't ask me to come to her mother's house, nor do I offer to visit. I suppose I should never have told her of Rolfe's threat, but, really, what else could I have done? Zoe's children are being cared for by her sister in Philadelphia. That's a mistake, I feel, but I'm in no position to offer advice. If I died, I'd want my kids at my funeral, but it's too late now. The children have already been shipped off.

Rolfe's funeral is strange. His parents live in Mexico and don't appear. He has no other living relatives; he has no friends. The Opthalmologists' Society sends a potted tree. Since everyone in the chapel is a friend of Zoe's, we look like a vast cheering section massed behind the widow, who sits in the front pew, looking neither happy nor sad. From far away, Zoe in black seems fragile and ethereal, all her vibrancy toned down.

As the clergyman gives a bland eulogy describing the virtues of a man no one can recognize, I try to summon up an image of Rolfe to give him a place at his funeral. All I can recall is his authoritative voice saying "wrong" when I suggested that suicide was hard to pull off. He must have been pleased with his cleverness. Didn't waste any time with Freudian analysis, Alcoholics Anonymous, marriage counseling. This time Zoe could not describe him as inept.

I sit alone toward the back of the chapel. Michael, who has been so comforting, is not with me. In the end he is as balky as ever. "I hate funerals, and I sure as hell don't know what to say to Zoe. Congratulations are inappropriate." I glared at him then, but now as I drift to the door after the service, I understand. I don't know what to say to Zoe either.

I've taken the day off from work—prepared to travel to the gravesite in a remote part of New Jersey. On the sidewalk in front of the funeral home I am surprised to find Zoe herself planted in the middle of the sidewalk directing traffic, pointing each mourner to her place. Up close she no longer looks ethereal but very much her aggressive self. She takes me firmly to her breast and grips me in a hard embrace.

"You don't have to come to the cemetery," she says, "I give you a dispensation."

I study her face, trying to find her feelings. Then I am stunned by the resentment I do find. After seven years I thought I knew Zoe, but I never really grasped her quintessence.

I feel betrayed. Unable to speak, I nod my head.

"Go home, Judy, go home. This is all too grim and ghastly. You still have a husband. Go home and enjoy him." As she enters her limousine, Zoe gives me a small and malicious smile.

An Old-fashioned Woman

She lives in Tarrytown with her husband, a harried advertising man. For a long time she has devoted herself to her three handsome children and handsome suburban house and has stopped taking good care of herself. Her hairstyle is flat and shapeless; she's given up wearing jewelry and perfume; her underwear is tattered. Once she was a stylish, good-looking woman, but who could tell that now? Let's call her Alice to protect her privacy.

One morning she wakes up in pain. A small bump on her back is greatly swollen. Although she's had this bump for months, when she pointed it out to her doctor during bronchitis last fall, he told her to leave it alone. "Why look for trouble?" were his exact words. Now she cannot sleep or move easily in the daytime.

Another painful night goes by, so first thing in the morning she calls the family dermatologist. Most people don't have a family dermatologist, but this thin-skinned family attracts all sorts of viruses and parasites. The little boy grew tiny red specks all over his thighs, which had to be burned off. The teenage girl had a loathsome rash all over her body for weeks before taking the SAT; the middle boy came home from camp with scabies. Alice herself had shingles and so did her husband, Jack, and there have been other things.

Alice has never particularly liked her dermatologist, who strikes her as coarse and insensitive. She prefers shy, sensitive people like herself. The doctor—Smith—is tall and balding with broad shoulders and a muscular build. He lacks intelligent small talk, and because the fair hair on his arms goes right down to his knuckles, he's always reminded her of a fairly intelligent ape. Still, those hairy fingers have cured the family ailments with a minimum of fuss, and although his practice has grown enormously, he still charges his faithful patients his old fees.

Irritated, in pain, Alice dials the office at 9:01 by her digital clock, but instead of the receptionist she expects at this hour, she hears a sleepy male voice.

"Is this Dr. Smith's office?" she asks.

"Oh, it's *you*," says the voice, unmistakably Dr. Smith's, in a rich, lazy tone. "Where have you gone to?"

Alice has been living a depressed suburban life for a long time, but she can recognize the overtones of sexual passion when she hears them.

"This is Dr. Smith's office, isn't it?" she repeats nervously. Dr. Smith (she understands the scenario at once) has been making love to a woman in his office; she visualizes the very couch in his consulting room. He has fallen heavily asleep; his lover has gone off, and now he thinks she has playfully telephoned him.

"It's Dr. Smith himself I'm speaking to, isn't it? How lucky to find you in," she continues with growing amusement. It is amusing to find your physician making a mistake, as long as it's not at your own expense. That her dermatologist, staid, balding, married, is playing around does not disturb Alice. He's not *her* husband, after all. "This is Mrs. Lowrey."

Dr. Smith instantly transforms himself. "I'm extremely sorry," he says in a brisk yet faintly embarrassed voice. "I was sure you were someone else. What's the trouble?"

Alice explains her condition, and they make an appointment for two o'clock that afternoon. Since she must pick up her son at the elementary school at three, he promises to get her out fast. Dr. Smith's office practices are admirable. He doesn't share his space with another doctor and keeps only two treatment rooms. One never finds more than one patient in his waiting room, which has bright lamps, sufficiently high chairs, and a No Smoking sign. His receptionist, Mrs. Biggs, is a sensible, middle-aged woman, not a doll.

At exactly two, Alice pulls her station wagon into the doctor's tiny parking lot. A funeral home stands directly across the road, a juxtaposition which might be damaging to a pediatrician, say, or to a surgeon, but which seems harmless enough for a dermatologist.

After greeting Mrs. Biggs, Alice, who has turned herself out neatly in a white blouse, tweed trousers, sensible walking shoes, and clean underwear, enters the empty waiting room and begins reading the *Smithsonian Magazine.* Only a few minutes later, she is summoned. She enters the treatment room, removes her blouse, lies down on the examining table on her tummy as directed.

"Ah, this is bad," says the doctor.

"I've had it for months. It was just a small bump."

"You should always have cysts looked at. They get infected."

"My internist said not to worry about it."

"That's because *he* didn't want to treat it."

They both smile at this cheerful cynicism.

Dr. Smith is looking very well since their last meeting, thin, energetic, almost rosy-cheeked. "It's the sex," Alice thinks to herself. She feels jealous. Her husband is a fine-looking, clever man who likes sex well enough but not when he is tired, depressed, or angry. These three states of mind, unfortunately, occupy most of his leisure hours.

Treatment consists of Dr. Smith leaning over Alice's back and squeezing the painful spot with all his might. "This is how I keep strong," he says in his familiar jocular vein. "Jocular" sounds like "jock," Alice thinks, trying to keep her mind off the pain.

"Am I hurting you?"

"No."

Dr. Smith is almost astride Alice now in his effort to expel the infection. Meanwhile she is steadfastly refusing to pay attention to the sexual implications of their situation. She has never been that type of woman. She's not going to start now. She doesn't think about Smith's mellow telephone voice; she ignores the fact that he is touching her bare skin, that she is only partially dressed. She derives satisfaction from the thought that her plain white bra is neither lacy nor low-cut. Mrs. Biggs must wear such a bra.

"How is your family?" Smith remarks as he pushes and strains against her.

"Well, all well."

"And your life? How is it going?"

"It's dreary," Alice finds herself replying. "It's very dreary, boring." She is utterly surprised at her response. She's never made this truthful comment to anyone.

Dr. Smith has finished his brutal work; he's walked over to his table and is fiddling with some surgical supplies. His back is to her. "Too bad," he says, far too lightheartedly.

Alice already regrets letting her feelings slip out. She wishes she'd kept both her cyst and her discontent to herself, had nursed the painful infection herself, hoping for spontaneous remission.

"You know what would cheer you up?" the doctor says suavely, his back still turned. "A matinee with me."

Alice may be mistaken, but she thinks she has just been propositioned. She is not being invited to see a play with the doctor. A matinee is a sexual encounter in the afternoon. She recognizes the term, though she doesn't know how she knows it. Where did she pick up this information? Surely not at the Parent Teachers Association or the Little League.

"That would be delightful," she finds herself saying in a pleased brittle voice, as though she's just been invited to a Heart Association luncheon.

Dr. Smith walks back behind her. "I'll need to see you in about a week's time. The dressing should be changed at least every other day, or more often if it gets messy. Can your husband do it?"

"He's squeamish." Alice feels treacherous in confessing this, although it's quite true. "But Jeffrey wants to be a doctor. He can change it."

"Smart boy." With lightning speed Dr. Smith is taping what seems an enormous area on her back. "Fine. Wonderful. There. Don't get it wet."

Alice awkwardly turns over on the examining table and sits up. In the jolt of moving she is able to look Dr. Smith in the face, his bland, everyday face. Surely she has just been hallucinating the remark about the matinee.

Dr. Smith stands close beside her, smiling. With one hairy forefinger he straightens the left strap of her bra, twisted all this time, in a casual possessive gesture.

"Let's try to find a mutually convenient time. What would it do to your schedule if you came in Monday early, say at 11:30? I'm booked in the afternoon and that would be more convenient for . . . picking up your son. Mrs. Biggs goes to lunch at 11:30, but I'll be back from the hospital by then."

Again Alice hears herself repeating, "That would be delightful," and she feels a sudden desire to laugh.

Until this point, Alice's story did not require a particular season of the year, but now that she leaves the doctor's office, the reader should be aware that it is February. Snow is on the ground, heaped on the side of the roadway and under the wheels of the station wagon. While Alice has been under treatment, however, a remarkable change in the weather has occurred, and as she steps out on the sidewalk she is astonished to find the sky brilliant blue, the trees and roofs melting, the pavement ankle-deep in slush.

Since it is only 2:25, Alice does not go directly to the elementary school but drives impromptu down the winding river road. The ice on the riverbank is breaking up. The few people she passes are smiling at the February thaw. It does seem as if all nature is rejoicing that she, Alice Lowrey, has been propositioned and has accepted. Instead of feeling degraded at the prospect of a loveless affair with her doctor (not an affair, she reminds herself; given the coolness of negotiations, the briefness of proposed duration, the clinical nature of the surroundings, it is not to be a romance but a simple sex act), Alice is overcome with joy.

Both the delight of secret keeping and the anticipation of pleasure make Alice exceptionally kind to her family that week. She confides in no one. Jack is the person she feels most drawn to tell ("Guess what! An amazing thing!"), but, of course, that is out of the question. If Dr. Smith were universally admired in the community, she might be tempted to tell her best friend, Anna, but what if Anna were to say, "That fellow? In his office? How gross!"

All week Alice dreamily returns in her imagination to the moment when Dr. Smith untwisted her bra strap. While at the actual moment she had no feeling but that of surprise, she now tries to describe to herself how she felt and recalls elusive images of passion.

Alice is also nervous, since she is not quite sure what the protocol of the occasion requires. For example, should she continue to address Smith by his medical title? Is she to wear her diaphragm?

For a timid woman there is no better lover than a medical doctor, for the skilled practitioner will be equal to whatever may occur. As a sense of this security penetrates Alice's brain, her jitters subside. At last she is able to leave home for her appointment feeling quite like herself but looking very much better than usual. She drives off with the feeling, happy in its simplicity, "Whatever happens, it won't be boring."

Just as she pulls her station wagon into her own snug parking space, Alice notes with surprise a woman emerging from Dr. Smith's front door. This unknown woman has not arrived by car; she makes her way on perilous high heels past Alice, who is still sitting in the driver's seat, and continues away from her in the direction of the village. Even in this one glimpse, Alice can see that the woman seems distressed. Her face is crumpled. Alice has the impression of a woman of something like her own age with something like her own coloring, but the face she sees looks worn and stricken, perhaps because the woman is wearing too much mascara and the mascara has dripped.

When the woman, who is dressed in a tightly belted fur coat, is almost out of sight, Alice, trembling with apprehension and excitement, slowly gets out of the car and goes up the steps.

At her ring, Dr. Smith himself opens the door, just as she imagined he would, but instead of supplying the lazy, amused or titillating remark she expected or the meaningful glance, the doctor stares past her head and speaks in a remote, nervous voice.

"Oh, Mrs. Lowrey, good. You're on time. I know you wanted to get out fast. Come along. It will only take a minute, if you're healing right."

Dazed, Alice follows Dr. Smith through one door and then another. As she passes the first narrow treatment room, she imagines she sees a bald-headed man sitting at a desk. At least she thinks it is a bald head and not a soup tureen or globe. She seems to have lost all mental alertness. In another minute she is lying on her tummy in the next room, hearing the snip, snip of the surgical scissors.

The greatest regret of her life is that she is presently wearing a black, low-cut bra.

Dr. Smith is behaving quite strangely. Instead of his usual silence interspersed with kind clichés, he is babbling incessantly. She tunes him in and out without gathering the thread of his discourse. He appears to be giving her moral pointers for the conduct of a disappointing life. "But you mustn't get depressed. It's awareness that's important . . . a positive viewpoint." All this in a very loud voice.

She keeps expecting him to bend down and whisper, "I'm sorry. We were interrupted," but since he doesn't, she knows she should demand an explanation. The idea of sex in a doctor's office, however, suddenly seems so utterly bizarre, the product of a disordered imagination, that she is thrown into silence. What if Dr. Smith had been inviting her to see *The Pi-rates of Penzance*? What made her imagine that she was a de-sirable woman?

Finally, dressed once more, she finds herself walking stonily past the adjoining room, into which she looks. The man next door is indeed a man and not a soup bowl. He sits bent over a pile of ledgers. She may assume that Dr. Smith's folksy ha-rangue was meant for his ears as well as for her own. But now the doctor accompanies her to the front door, which is proba-bly out of the stranger's earshot, and now is the moment when he will explain his conduct. Perhaps he will ask for another appointment.

But the matinee of her imagination is forever beyond reach, as Dr. Smith shakes her hand and says with a rare, friendly smile of relief, "I know I'll be seeing you again one of these days. Good luck—" and sends her out, as if with a kick, into the cold February air.

Here we must draw the curtain over the rest of her story. Alice's grief and shame are too ugly for the general public. In time she will judge herself less harshly, but she doesn't know that now. Let's allow her to feel humiliated in the privacy of her home without the pity or scorn of strangers.

Free Writing

September 28

What am I doing here, trapped in a grammar class? It would be worse if I weren't the teacher. Students bent over your ragged notebook paper, do you know who you are, and where we are going? Free writing means writing whatever comes into your head. Don't let those pencils slip off your damp little scraps. Don't stop; don't think. If you get blocked, just repeat the same words till you break through.

Free writing will set your creative juices flowing. That's what Mildred, Director of Composition, said. And even if it doesn't, it takes up ten minutes of this interminable remedial hour. Wastes ten minutes, that's what I say, me, Fortune's free-writing fool—eleven years of experience teaching my guts out, but not the Director of Composition, no, not me. Many are called but few are chosen. We also serve who only sit here till ten o'clock at night in this windowless building. Teaching the Unteachable. Reaching the Unreachable. It's OK if you really want to do it. But I don't really want to do it.

Must keep busy scribbling, though. Theme paper, smooth, white, available at any stationery store. It's the third night of the term, for god's sake, and how many students made it to a stationery store? Two out of twenty. My brain cells are popping one by one, and if I find free writing hard, how are you faring, poor bastards?

May Mildred be smashed with heavy thesauruses, smitten with semicolons, crushed by colons. If I get the chance, I'll wring her shallow chicken's neck. False, smug, self-righteous, hypocritical. Oh for a stream of icicles freezing her face! Oh dull housewife with a duplicating machine! She brags like a horse. She's teaching Romantic Poetry tonight in this very building, upstairs where there are snot-green industrial carpets, very chic, while I labor in a bare room, formerly an animal laboratory, drain in the middle of the floor, air conditioning booming off the formica like Victoria Falls.

I fancy I hear Mildred's grating voice through the ceiling,

shredding the Odes. Faint melodies are sweet but those un-
heard are sweeter. I fast, I faint, I die, I try. If you don't like my
harmonica, don't blow it. If you don't like my harmonica, don't
blow it.

Stop this nonsensical parody of the only world the world
has ever known. Get on with your class, Miss Thirty-Two-Year-
Old Free Writer. Start the semicolons rolling.

September 30

Now, ladies and gentlemen, ten minutes ago I was crying in
the toilet of the East Science Facility. Would that interest you if
you knew it? Spinster schoolteacher, tough old birdy, meets
long-lost lover in dim corridors of the East Science Facility. Almost knocks him over, in fact, since she, always buxom, has
gotten very tubby in her loneliness and frustration, and he, always on the small side, has gotten weedy thin in whatever sick
situation he's creating nowadays. Separation obviously isn't
good for either of these birds, but after two years do they fall
into each other's arms and cuddle, crying, "Well-met, well-
met," all hugs and kisses and echoes of old ecstasies?

No, sirs and mesdames, they are cold. "How are you, Ivor?"
Cold, cold. "Teaching one course while working on your dissertation?" Fine, good. Still working on your bloody dissertation. Too much screwing; one's vital juices stop flowing. (You
told me *I* was preventing you from finishing your dissertation,
dog, remember?)

"You, Helaine? Still working on your novel?" Sure, pal,
would you like to see it? I've got it here in my back pocket. Just
dash it off by candlelight after teaching four overcrowded
composition courses. A chapter a day keeps the doctor away.
Beats masturbation.

Do we exchange confidences? Relive old frolics? Review
lusty quarrels and juicy brawls? No, we chat coldly. You look as
distinguished as ever, Ivor. Do you still wear tattered underwear? Still shower with a cap on, like a girl? Still thrash around

in your bed like a sardine? Publish essays in the *Pisspot Review*?

Perhaps you saw me crying, sisters. Through the mile-wide crack in the toilet door. I was in the cubicle that locks, sobbing into the corrugated toilet paper. I saw you, Charlene, standing in the spot of peril by the mirror (miraculous gray hair detector), getting cracked by the door each time it opened. You gave me a searching anthropologist's look. Some tribes would rather be seen peeing than crying. I pretended to have a heavy cold, my stiff upper lip like a handball court.

Oh Ivor, why didn't you just put your hand on my cheek and say, "There, there, old duck. If you lose some weight, you can hold out another fifty years?" Or why didn't I just silently kiss your hand?

We want to be happy, but how are we going to do it? My class wants to be happy, but how are they going to do it? We want to be loved, but how are we going to do it?

These questions ask themselves.

October 5

Awake, sluggards! Cast off your multiple choice exams. Throw your textbooks out the window. (But there are no windows here—no matter.) Anoint yourselves with salad oil. Put on your royal bathrobes; the feast of meaningless mistakes is about to begin.

How I wish I had a little cookie to nibble on, meanwhile. To compose myself as I compose. Make little announcements. See all those sleeping, swaying heads bounce up.

"Class, I'm taking next week off to be with my lover. We're locking ourselves in the slop closet with a twelve-pack.

"I'm planning to set myself afire. Forget about the theme paper. Please bring unleaded gasoline.

"No, better, I'm planning to set your assignments afire. If you want the ashes, you must give me a stamped, self-addressed envelope by Thursday night."

Peter Heinz is absent tonight. Peter Heinz is absent; so is José Pereirra and John Incremona. I don't think you can pass the course, young man. Why not, sir or madame? Because you're stupid.

Where is my plagiarist? There he is, slumped in the back row under the coats. A weedy blond. Butter wouldn't melt the scoundrel. Did he think that I'd believe those fine, sensitive moments occurred in *his* childhood? And that sublime final image, the blue rubber ball disappearing into the cloudless sky never to be seen again. A bit of poetry in English 1.5. David Gold with the golden hair. A long history of thievery, I'll wager. Absent from the first impromptu essay, clever dog, and planning to be absent from all future impromptus. A strong, solid style, a little better than Orwell's. A maniac's handwriting. Absurd technical errors (like missing capitals) unimaginatively sprinkled here and there. I'll track this plagiarist down if it's the last thing I do. Catch him inky-fingered. Nail him at the Xerox. I will not be tricked by a stripling. I'll try Orwell first. Haunt the libraries. Leave no stack unturned.

"How pleasant it is at the end of the day / No follies to have to repent / But reflect on the past and be able to say / My time has been properly spent."

October 7

Full Professor, step right in; take a seat in the back. My guardian and my observer, observe me, yes. An amazing display of talent—no relaxation but lots of nervous tension and anxiety to make you feel at home. I'd strip myself naked for you, Stranger, but how will you get it in your Evaluation Report?

"We generally do ten minutes of free writing right at the start to let the creative juices flow, heh, heh, heh."

Such tact! Such wit! Fly with me to the blackboard and see how we go. The true thrill—grade a paper with me. Watch me stalk sentence fragments, pounce on wordy constructions, disport myself among awkward tenses, linger on those ever-loving concrete details. I want to caution you about one thing, however. I always put observers on my Death List.

He looks pretty bored, my keen observer, lolling in the back row, playing with his pencil. No learning takes place here, Buster. Why don't you try an auto school?

October 14

Walking to school from the bus stop today—unspeakable happiness. I floated! I sang! And why?

Because David Gold is alive. He walks, he talks, he exists on this planet. He is sitting before me now, holding his head in his hands, not free writing a bit. All I can see is a grubby green sleeve and some golden hair.

Dear boy. You are my booster cable. I thought my heart had gone dead long ago, but for good or bad, you recharged it for me.

It was his turn for a conference. He sat sideways by my desk, with his lanky legs folded twice over, staring at the blackboard. He had been late; he didn't seem to be listening. I couldn't mention his plagiarism until I had some evidence, and in my frustration I let my contempt show too plainly.

"Losing that rubber ball must have left a big hole in your life," said I scornfully. "Do you always omit capital letters at the beginning of sentences, or do you do it just for me? Have you ever thought of attending Handwriting School?"

He looked straight at me for the first time, flushing, and one bright tear rolled out of one eye. At that moment the rest of the class came piling into the room. "I'll talk to you about this later," I said, turning toward the others. "We're going to write impromptu tonight," I told them impulsively.

They shrank back with well-known groaning noises. "It's not fair. . . ." "Why didn't you tell us?"

"Then it wouldn't be impromptu." I smiled encouragingly.

"Don't be afraid. It's only one paragraph." Only your native language. I hurriedly wrote a topic on the board.

Meanwhile David moved back to his seat, turned his plastic chair around to the wall, tucked his head down to his chest, and sat in that furious hidden posture until I called for their work. All the while I sat there, watching him, half-suspecting his paper was going to be blank.

As soon as the classroom was safely cleared, I plucked his impromptu from the pile. One and a half closely scribbled sheets. Describe a concrete object concretely. Almost impossible for a remedial student. I was a sadist to assign it.

David described his Harley-Davidson so crisply I could see it shining before me on the sidewalk. (Still no capitals, but editors can always fix up that sort of thing.) I thought—perhaps he had this magnificent paragraph up his sleeve, would have written about motorcycles no matter what the topic. Perhaps he had assorted plagiarisms stuffed in all the pockets of his jeans. Then I remembered the single rolling tear and his scarlet, vulnerable face, the fury in his hunched-over neck. I read the paragraph again, savoring it. I felt an unfamiliar yet well-known stirring in my chest. (All great things are clichés.) I felt joy swelling up, or perhaps it was pain. Felt something, anyway, instead of dead. I remembered the last time I felt my heart move. I was sitting in the front seat of Ivor's car, parked for a long time in the snow. "You don't seem to understand. I'll put it more plainly," he said. "I don't want to see you anymore."

I will purify myself for David's sake. I will better my life. David Gold exists. For no other reason, I rejoice.

October 19

A class of five. Five little blackbirds sitting on a branch. My brilliant one is not among them.

George, your work has not been good. Achilles, your work has not been good. Everyone else, your work has not been good.

Nobody's work is any good. Except for my darling.
I had today:

2 cups coffee with real milk
1 toast with diet butter
1 midget bagel with peanut butter
1 cup Bran Buds with skim milk
1 roast beef sandwich with lettuce & tomato & a cup of tea

That's not too much. A penitential menu. When I come home, I will have:

1 cup decaffeinated coffee with real milk
1 piece of deskinned chicken, broiled

That will truly be delicious. That's not asking too much. Who am I to ask too much?

He has a girlfriend. How could I have not noticed it? She waits for him every Tuesday and Thursday evening right outside in the hallway beside the elevator. She is short, size three, I'd say, young and nondescript. When he emerges, she falls comfortably into place at his side like his hunting dog, and the elevator closes slowly upon them. They never speak. They are shy. Their utterances are too significant for the general public. She is a deaf mute. How will I ever know what the answer is? Why do I want to know in the first place?

They are probably necking in the backseat of a car right now, her head pillowed on his grammar. No, I am hopelessly outdated. They are screwing.

I am glad he has a girlfriend. I am glad he is screwing.

Face it, Helaine. Don't be a fraud. It's not just that he is a fine student with a good mind whom I will be glad to recommend for the Nobel Prize. Not that he's shy and humiliated and at my mercy. He also has rosy skin and long muscular legs in tight pants. He is a beautiful, desirable young man. And I desire him.

October 21

All you can eat and doughnuts, too. A steaming cup of hot coffee and a cracker. A bowl of chili, reddening your mouth. Plenty of fresh milk and cookies. Sesame crackers and small kegs of beer. Tree-ripened pears with russet flecks on them. Cider and doughnuts. Hot tomato soup with six oyster crackers tumbling on the surface. A bacon, lettuce, and tomato sandwich crunching crisp, especially the lettuce. No soggy greens, please. Two mugs of fresh coffee with cream. A peppermint stick ice cream cone. Twelve cinnamon buns with jelly inside. A hogshead of cream cheese, one-half pound smoked Scotch salmon, and two dozen bagels. Chilled caviar, black ripe Greek olives. Dainty little cucumber sandwiches with the crusts cut off. Rum mulled with cider. A barrel of pickled herring with fresh onion curls. Carrot sticks as a refreshment. Cold Heineken beer, oysters, beets with pickles, a bit of salami and cold tongue on fresh bakery rolls with onion and a quarter pound of sweet butter. Freshly scrambled eggs and toast and a very tiny little bit of ketchup. I give up all of these for you, my chicken.

October 26

I can't help thinking someone is out to get me.

Could it be me? Am I out to get me?

This time I arranged our conference better. Little seminar room not used at this hour. Thirty minutes before class time so we won't be interrupted. I have emptied my papers on the table to give the little cell a homier look. I have muted the air conditioning. I have put his last essay with a big red A in magic marker on top of the pile. Everything to put him at his ease.

He is not at his ease. He does have a pleasant sweet odor about him, which I can't quite place. He has crossed his legs more gracefully this time, but he's still looking at me as though I'm about to take a bite from his rosy flesh. He thinks I am a meat-eating dinosaur—ferocious Tyrannosaurus rex—when I am really a shy, love-sick Brontosaurus—huge vegetarian with a marshmallow heart.

"You are a talented writer," I begin. "What are you doing in this remedial class?"

"I failed the proficiency exam. Do you think I'm taking this class for fun?" He is still angry with me. He speaks in a thin, waspish, bratty young man's voice. "I failed it three times, if you want to know."

I try not to be insulted. I hate English 1.5, too, so why should I be insulted? Am I teaching it for fun? "You must get terrifically nervous, then," I say kindly.

"I don't know."

"Well, there must be something on your mind when you take the exam."

"I think it's because my mother works here."

Oh, I think. I visualize the refugee daughter of a great philosopher, scrubbing floors in the library. Blond braids pinned upon aristocratic head. All hopes pinned on her son. "Does your mother expect you to do very well? Is that why you're nervous?"

"*You* know my mother. She teaches in this department." A petulant smile tweaks his mouth for an instant before he drops his dynamite. "Mildred Gold." Director of Composition. Administrator of proficiency exams.

The son of Mildred. In a flash I understand everything. Omission of capital letters is, after all, a reasonable act for the son of Mildred. He does pretty much what he wants. Revenge is his reason for living. Does poorly in school because it irritates her. Is lazy. Has gotten everything he's ever wanted. Psychologically unsteady. Poor boy.

Also oddly, in the same flash I understand something about myself. Humiliation is the root of the attraction, but it's *my* humiliation, not his. Humiliating for a grown woman to care about a boy. And now that I know whose boy it is . . . I feel self-disgust oozing up.

He lives in the home of my enemy. Empties her garbage. Shovels the snow on her front walk. Walks her poodle. I've lost all respect for myself. How can I care for the fetcher and carrier of Mildred's petty household domain? Her bootblack.

He was once a speck in her ovaries; he passed down through her birth canal, squeezing her bladder. She wiped his baby ass for him, and he vomited over her when he was sick. These sordid custodial details notwithstanding, he now has the power to hurt me, that is, I now love him desperately. I am helpless and angry, but my fine old poker face does not betray me. From outside I appear calm and beneficent, not even very much surprised.

"It must be hard for you to study a subject your mother teaches, in a program she directs. Why don't you switch to another school?"

"She won't allow it. It's inconvenient."

"What about your father?"

"My stepfather. He does whatever she wants. She's a very powerful woman."

Admiring (spurious) smile on both our faces. Mildred. What do I really know about her? She is always rallying others to her causes. Collecting money for the Big Chairman's wedding present (third marriage, why bother?). Appeals and posters clutter her office. Sauvez les Trésors de la Nubie. Rettet die Schatze aus Nubien. Salvad los Tresoros de Nubia. Prevent new coal gasification plants in Navajo Territory. Save our Football Field. Ban the Bomb. Robert Frost's sappy face beams over her shoulder. None of this good work seems native to her. Everything's a front. She works hard to seem good-natured. Her hostile, stupid eyes twinkle from behind her aviator frames. For some reason, she hates me.

"I could speak to her about it. You really don't belong in a remedial class. You must know it."

He gives me a blank look. A marble-eyed look of elegant Greek statues. Antinoüs, the Emperor's favorite, whom I also fell for once at Olympia.

"Of course, I'm very glad to have you in my class," I say warmly. "I like brilliant people."

Whatever made me think he was diffident? He accepts my declaration with bland indifference. His royal due. "I was thinking of going out west," he remarks.

"Next summer?"

"Next month."

"Oh, please, David. Don't do anything precipitously."

"I'm going by motorcycle. If I go, I have to do it before it's too cold."

"Does your mother know about this?"

He gives me an "Are you kidding?" look.

"How are you doing in your other courses?"

He looks pleased. Glad I asked. "I'm failing two, math and sociology, and an A-plus so far in the other, in Ivor Braun's class. He wants me to major in Comparative Literature. And I don't know about your class."

"C," I say, just to shake his self-image a little. Exactly like Ivor to give out A-pluses at midterm, then let you down hard at the end with a B. Did the same to me once. "You deserve an A, David, for content and general style, and an F, of course, for punctuation. But if you sat down for twenty minutes and read your grammar book . . . Why didn't your mother tell me about your problem? I see her every day."

"She wants me to be independent."

"I'll bet."

I say it out loud, sarcastically. He doesn't flinch. He doesn't blush. His eyes are green and filled with contact lenses. I hate to mention how long his eyelashes are.

"Don't speak to her about it, please," he says seriously. "Just pass me. That's all I need."

"How old are you, David?"

"Twenty-one." He grins, ashamed.

"So old?" Only eleven years between us. Dr. Johnson's wife was at least twenty years older. He was inconsolable when she died, but kept right on writing his dictionary.

"I dropped out once before, when I was in high school." He leans forward a little, as if telling a secret. I'm enjoying his lovely fragrance. "My mother got me a job with Scribner's, as an office boy."

I think more about Mildred, what it must be like to live under her benevolent direction. I can't imagine what it must be like.

Mildred wears a lot of makeup. She articulates poorly. One of her mimeographed notices began, "Due to a lack of examination booklets. . . ." I guess you could say she is vulgar for an academic or academic for a vulgarian. She takes a housewifely interest in paper clips, envelopes, and exam books. She is the chatelaine of the supply closet.

At the end of each semester, Mildred collects a set of essays from one student, chosen at random from each class. They must be submitted in a lightweight, soft-covered binder with metal fasteners. She reads through the papers and makes some trenchant comment. Last term mine said, "Fine!" The semester before that, there was no exclamation point, so I guess I've improved. A few years ago, I taught Creative Writing, which I rather enjoyed, but Mildred thinks I do better with Composition. "We need good people in Remediation," she said good-naturedly. She likes to be chummy. When I stopped seeing Ivor, she said, "I see you've stopped seeing Ivor." When I lost the office key, she said, "Do try and be more careful with this one. I know you're an artist and have published a book, and all that, but . . ."

It's 9:30. The class is looking at me a little bit cross-eyed; they're tired of writing. David is smiling at me from way back there, flirtatiously peeking at me from under his hands. It's a kind of sweet blackmailing smile, a buddylike smile, most unsuitable for student-teacher relationships. I know you know I'm a gem, that smile says. I've revealed my true identity, like Billy Batson. What are you going to do for me now?

I will close up shop. One final thought occurs to me: the ultimate humiliation. That pleasant, sweet odor I liked so much was, oh help, bubblegum.

October 28

Tonight an unusual show: Ivor and David together. Standing together at the front of the lunchroom, they canceled out each other's good looks. Ivor, of course, seemed much older; next to David's bright head his gray hairs suddenly stuck out stiffly, like brush bristles. He seemed worn, stained, as though seen through a muddy filter. David, on the other hand, without Ivor's authority, looked white and pasty, like a pie taken out of the oven too soon.

I had a clear view but couldn't hear at all. They seemed to be speaking pleasantly enough, but urgently. Why were they all standing up? This was no passing chatter. At one point David thrust out his hands in the incongruous shrug of a Yiddish peddler. He couldn't account for something. What the hell was it? I was torn by curiosity but kept flicking my eyes back and forth mock-casually and, desperate to see, purposely blocked my vision with my upthrust coffee cup. It occurred to me, as it often does, that someone else in the lunchroom might be watching me. I determined to betray nothing to the unknown watcher but felt on reflection that I must look like a frantic bunny, my head swiveling, eyes swimming, my mouth still chewing wildly my already swallowed food. But of course there was no one looking and nothing to be seen.

Oh yes, I forgot to mention that David's girl was present throughout the colloquy, standing silently at his elbow. She impressed me as usual as being very short (She always seems only to come up to David's elbow. His elbow stands out in these scenes), very dowdy, and vaguely nice. Naturally I never focus on her, as my eyes are engaged elsewhere. I would not recognize her alone.

When the conversation, which took about three minutes, was over, David and the girl walked briskly out of the lunchroom. Now something strange happened, which I have read about in books but never experienced before. Either David put his arm around her as she trotted along at his elbow or else he didn't. I, an alert type, watching with the fixed seriousness of a U.N. observer, am uncertain. Perhaps they flowed along so smoothly, so adhesively that it looked as though they were connected by an arm, and I seized on this false dramatic detail to remember. Or perhaps there was an arm, and even as I looked at it (this is what I have read about in books), I was unwilling to see it.

November 4

I am not even on campus. I am on Main Street in front of the public library, at least three miles away, when I hear the zoom of a motorcycle. The chances that this will be David are 7,000 to 1, but these days I am thrown into a frenzy by the sight of any motorcycle. It's the ambiguous figure of the helmeted, goggled rider that throws me—the masked rider of the plains. This time the figure I imagine is David *is* David. It must be, because the rider in back is Mildred.

The bike pulls up to the curb for a moment, and she hops off, spry as you please in her denim pantsuit. She's a pretty high kicker for a woman her age; you have to give her credit. Goes to the health club three times a week and steams herself to a pulp. Takes yoga, too. I saw her chuffing away in the lunchroom once, noisily demonstrating how to expel poisonous, used-up air from the lungs. She sent a little poisonous stream my way.

As David roars off, I try melting back against the library wall, but she's spotted me. She hails me excitedly. I wonder whether to bring up David's problems, but, as usual, subtlety is not a requisite with Mildred.

"Well, are you going to pass him?" she asks.

"Mildred," I say diffidently. "Why don't you send your son to another school? It can't be good for him to study under your shadow, so to speak."

Her powerful carbon-arc eyes shoot me a furious look through her glasses, but her mouth continues smiling benevolently. "He's not failing, is he?"

"Mildred," I begin again, "I won't fail him unless he forces me to do it. The trouble is—he's stopped doing his assignments. How can I pass him if he doesn't write anything?"

"Well, I thought if anybody could handle him, you could, Helaine. I can't make him write. I haven't been able to make him do anything since he was toilet trained." She laughs raucously. "What he does and when he does it are a mystery to me. He has his own apartment over the garage. He has his own transportation, his own stereo. You don't know what it's like to have a teenage son these days."

"If David doesn't like college work, maybe he should just be cut loose. He's not really a teenager anymore, is he?"

Mildred is really furious with me now. Or is she in pain? Her face has creased badly in a spasm of some emotion; it's hard for me to tell.

"We've tried that already. He quit a good job in publishing to work at a soda fountain."

The image of David in the guise of a soda jerk is as painful to me as it is to Mildred, but for different reasons. Perhaps he has waited on me in a comic-book cap, and I've thought him negligible.

"Helaine, Davey is beyond my control. That's what I'm trying to tell you. How will he get along without his diploma? He can't stay in my garage forever. And he used to be such a bright, cheerful kid." Mildred's voice is breaking. She is actually weeping, her eyes glazed over. She is metamorphosing before my eyes from department tyrant to bereaved parent, and I resent it. Dammit, Mildred, stop sniveling. Stalin worried about his teenagers, too, perhaps.

November 9

He did not come for our conference tonight. He did not give me any assignments. He entered the room all tousled, rain-bedraggled, his jeans soaked up to the knee. Perhaps he'd been stuck on the highway. "David," I called out cheerfully. "You look as though you waded to class." He stalked past my desk, avoiding my eyes.

I rather expected it. Screw you, he's saying. You claim to be my admirer and friend. Prove it. Pass me no matter what I do. Fail me, and I'll go west. Go ahead, wreck my academic career.

I had a fantasy about him the other night. A daydream, that is, I was controlling it. I dreamed he came to my apartment for tea. I dusted especially for him. I bought two cakes from the Dumas Pâtisserie, and I took my Tabriz carpet out of hock.

He brought grass, special high-quality Acapulco Gold, and we sat on the carpet, sharing a joint. In my dream he wore a fuzzy woolen sweater of an unusual orange, something pumpkinlike but more pleasant. All colors were sharp because of the imaginary grass, and I felt myself leaning imperceptibly toward him, till I felt the sweater fuzz against my bare neck. We were listening to Chopin, *Valse Brilliante.*

You think this was prelude to an erotic fantasy? He stroked my neck, I slowly unbuttoned my blouse, my nipples popped out, he unzipped his pants. You are wrong, quite wrong. You know me very little. In my dream I never forgot he was David. In my dream we simply sat in a deep passionate calm; Artur Rubinstein was doing all the work. Then David said solemnly, "Thank you, Helaine, for a very happy moment. Don't get up; stay with the music." He left the package of grass on the table and went away, and I never saw him again.

November 16

He is absent again. He is not here tonight. He is absent again. He is not here tonight.

Freewriting freewriting freewriting because I'm so afraid. I have to hold my face together.

She came in, the girl, just now while I was writing, and said, "Here are David Gold's assignments. He's sorry they're so late."

I stare at her. "Where is David?"

"He said please excuse the handwriting. He was nervous; he had to write them on his wedding day."

"His wedding day!"

She giggles. "We were married this morning at City Hall and tomorrow, if he finishes his paper for Comp. Lit., we're going to California." She giggles again, a cheerful young girl.

I stare at her harder. She looks wholesome, a nice friendly face, too nice for him. She's wearing a useful gray jumper. She should be wearing alençon lace with a bouquet of stephanotis and sweet peas. From the back of a motorcycle she hurls her bouquet.

I hold the envelope steadily in my hand. "You're going by motorcycle?"

"No, by plane. His mother gave us the tickets as a wedding present. We were going to go at Christmas, but we decided not to wait."

The people in the front row have stopped writing and are looking at us curiously. Up till now I have never let anyone, not even my observer, interrupt my free writing.

"Now that he is up to date . . ." She has a soft voice. Her enunciation is very good. "David wants to know, can you please give him an Incomplete grade? We'll be back next semester."

The result of this question is that I begin shaking from the waist down at my desk, as if I have palsy. My legs are trembling so violently, I have to keep shuffling my feet, as though something unpleasant has stuck to my shoes. I can also feel myself blushing, but to my astonishment, the girl doesn't notice a thing. Of course. The desk has a little skirt around it for modesty's sake.

"Why doesn't David come and ask me himself?"

"He can't. He's writing this paper for Comp. Lit. And I think he's embarrassed."

Now that I look at her, I recognize her from the front desk of the library. She has checked me out many times. I wish to say,

"It is highly irregular to give the grade of Incomplete except in cases of serious illness or a death in the family," but the words seem like bullets, and I can't mouth them. Instead I put the envelope in my briefcase, and I nod, smiling. I clear my throat, I croak a little, I say, "Have a good time." As she exits, smiling, I see she is taller than I had thought. I still don't know her name.

This happened one minute ago. I already feel a little remote from it. I am planning to resume my normal life. My mouth has already frozen back to its normal shape. My legs have stopped trembling. No one could tell how I feel.

How I wish I could start all over again as a tadpole. Something small swimming around in a sea. Something squirreling along.

I don't know what to do. I don't know what to say. I don't know where to go. The door is blank. The wall is blind. The floor has a drain.

The mouse lurks in the pantry. Garbage roots in the backyard. Birds fly in the circular sky.

Don't relax for a minute. Make sure you sleep at night. Give a knock if you exist. No knock if you don't. Nod your head if you can breathe. Forget me. Forget me not.

November 18

Another opening, another show.

Another opening, another show. Another opening, another show.

Another opening, another show. Another opening, another show.

Another opening, another show. Another opening. Another show.

Other Iowa Short Fiction Award and John Simmons Short Fiction Award Winners

1990
A Hole in the Language,
Marly Swick
Judge: Jayne Anne Phillips

1989
Lent: The Slow Fast,
Starkey Flythe, Jr.
Judge: Gail Godwin

1989
Line of Fall, Miles Wilson
Judge: Gail Godwin

1988
The Long White,
Sharon Dilworth
Judge: Robert Stone

1988
The Venus Tree,
Michael Pritchett
Judge: Robert Stone

1987
Fruit of the Month, Abby Frucht
Judge: Alison Lurie

1987
Star Game, Lucia Nevai
Judge: Alison Lurie

1986
Eminent Domain, Dan O'Brien
Judge: Iowa Writers' Workshop

1986
Resurrectionists, Russell Working
Judge: Tobias Wolff

1985
Dancing in the Movies,
Robert Boswell
Judge: Tim O'Brien

1984
Old Wives' Tales,
Susan M. Dodd
Judge: Frederick Busch

1983
Heart Failure, Ivy Goodman
Judge: Alice Adams

1982
Shiny Objects, Dianne Benedict
Judge: Raymond Carver

1981
The Phototropic Woman,
Annabel Thomas
Judge: Doris Grumbach

1980
Impossible Appetites,
James Fetler
Judge: Francine du Plessix Gray

1979
Fly Away Home, Mary Hedin
Judge: John Gardner

1978
A Nest of Hooks, Lon Otto
Judge: Stanley Elkin

1977
The Women in the Mirror,
Pat Carr
Judge: Leonard Michaels

1976
The Black Velvet Girl,
C. E. Poverman
Judge: Donald Barthelme

1975
*Harry Belten and the
Mendelssohn Violin Concerto,*
Barry Targan
Judge: George P. Garrett

1974
*After the First Death There Is
No Other,* Natalie L. M. Petesch
Judge: William H. Gass

1973
The Itinerary of Beggars,
H. E. Francis
Judge: John Hawkes

1972
The Burning and Other Stories,
Jack Cady
Judge: Joyce Carol Oates

1971
*Old Morals, Small Continents,
Darker Times,*
Philip F. O'Connor
Judge: George P. Elliott

1970
The Beach Umbrella,
Cyrus Colter
Judges: Vance Bourjaily
and Kurt Vonnegut, Jr.